WINNIE NASH IS *NOT* YOUR SUNSHINE

ALSO BY NICOLE MELLEBY

Hurricane Season

In the Role of Brie Hutchens . . .

How to Become a Planet

The Science of Being Angry

Camp QUILTBAG (with A. J. Sass)

Sunny and Oswaldo

SUNRISE LAGOON 1: Sam Makes a Splash

SUNRISE LAGOON 2: Marina in the Middle

WINNIE NASH IS *NOT* YOUR SUNSHINE

Nicole Melleby

ALGONQUIN YOUNG READERS
WORKMAN PUBLISHING
NEW YORK

Algonquin Young Readers
Workman Publishing
Hachette Book Group, Inc.
1290 Avenue of the Americas
New York, NY 10104
workman.com

Algonquin Young Readers is an imprint of Workman Publishing, a division of
Hachette Book Group, Inc. The Algonquin Young Readers name and logo are
registered trademarks of Hachette Book Group, Inc.

Design by Carla Weise

The publisher is not responsible for websites (or their content) that are not
owned by the publisher.

Workman books may be purchased in bulk for business, educational, or promotional
use. For information, please contact your local bookseller or the Hachette Book Group
Special Markets Department at special.markets@hbgusa.com.

Library of Congress Cataloging-in-Publication Data

Names: Melleby, Nicole, author.
Title: Winnie Nash is not your sunshine / Nicole Melleby.
Description: First edition. | New York : Algonquin Young Readers, 2024. |
Audience: Ages 9–12. | Audience: Grades 4–6. |
Summary: Winnie Nash, who has been keeping her sexual orientation a secret, spends the
summer with her grandma in New Jersey as she struggles with her family's expectations
while yearning to embrace her true self and attend the Pride Parade in New York City.
Identifiers: LCCN 2023032949 | ISBN 9781643753133 (hardcover) |
ISBN 9781523527458 (ebook)
Subjects: CYAC: Grandparent and child—Fiction. | Grandmothers—Fiction. |
Identity—Fiction. | LGBTQ+ people—Fiction. | LCGFT: Novels.
Classification: LCC PZ7.1.M46934 Wi 2024 | DDC [Fic]—dc23
LC record available at https://lccn.loc.gov/2023032949

First Edition April 2024 LSC-C

Printed in the United States of America on responsibly sourced paper.

10 9 8 7 6 5 4 3 2 1

To Jim,
who loved this book fiercely enough
to keep me from shelving it.

And to Minna,
who taught me how to find strength
in the stories that make me who I am.

PART ONE

PRIDE (NOUN):

a feeling of deep pleasure or satisfaction derived from one's own achievements, the achievements of those with whom one is closely associated, or from qualities or possessions that are widely admired.

ONE

WINNIE SAT SMACK-DAB IN THE MIDDLE OF A GROUP OF NOSY senior citizens with a scowl on her face. They were discussing her name, instead of the book they were there for.

"It says *Winnifred* Nash. I just assumed she was one of us! Can you blame me?"

"You know what they say about assuming. You make an—"

"Shh! Watch your mouth around the child!"

"This is why I vote that she goes. I don't want to have to censor myself. It's really not fair, you know."

"You don't need to censor yourself," Winnie

chimed in, still scowling. "And are you going to keep talking about me or can we start this stupid book club and talk about the actual book."

Winnie's grandma would scold her for talking to them like that. But Winnie's grandma was the reason she was here in the first place, was the reason for a lot of things weighing on Winnie's chest, so, really, she didn't care what her grandma wanted. Her grandma was currently in a heated game of canasta, which Winnie hated. Mostly because Winnie was terrible at it. But her grandma refused to let Winnie stay home alone—even though she was twelve, not five, and home was now her grandma's house, which was literally across the street from the community clubhouse.

From three to four every weekday, Winnie's grandma played canasta. So, from three to four every weekday, Winnie was forced to go with her.

Winnie's dad both worried and worked around the clock, and her mom was working (causing her dad more worry) a lot lately, too. And since school was out for the summer, and Winnie didn't have anything else to do, she was sent an hour away to stay with her grandmother, even though no one asked Winnie what she wanted to do. Her parents said they needed the time to "deal with some things." Which meant Winnie's grandma was left to deal with *her*, and vice versa.

"The clubhouse" sounded fancier than what it was. It was really just a scuffed-up and overused auditorium with some tables, a few couches, a ton of folding chairs, and a single unisex bathroom that smelled like a mix of Vicks VapoRub and peppermint and pee.

On her third visit to the clubhouse, after declaring canasta the *worst card game ever!*, Winnie had sulked in the corner, prepared to frown and wait in silence until it was time to cross the street back home. She'd been frowning a lot lately. Which was fine, because then Winnie's mom could keep all the smiles for herself.

But on that third visit, while Winnie sulked in the corner, she shifted in an uncomfortable metal folding chair and managed to knock over a stack of books on the table next to her. She'd sighed, continued to frown, and picked up the books to restack them.

The cover of one was colorful and flowery and elegant. The kind of cover that ends up with an Oprah or Reese Witherspoon book club sticker on it.

Winnie figured it was probably some dumb romance. That was what old people read, wasn't it?

Something with a tall, dark, and handsome man. Winnie didn't care much for tall, dark, and handsome men.

But she'd had an hour to kill.

And a dumb romance novel was better than canasta.

Which was why, after what turned into an hour and a half of waiting for her grandma to be ready to leave, Winnie had held on to the book. And she'd added her name to the Book Club Sign-Up Sheet.

Winnifred Maude Nash.

A fitting name for a senior citizen book club. Because of this, no one questioned it, until she'd shown up, tall but still twelve. The actual senior citizen members of the book club had no idea what to do with her.

"So?" Winnie spoke up. "Are we gonna talk about this book or not?"

The answer, apparently, was *not*, as they continued discussing (more like arguing about) her, right in front of her. Which, really, she was pretty used to ever since her mom had lost her smiles, but it just made Winnie extra mad. She stood abruptly, uncomfortable folding chair screeching against the worn hardwood floor. "Fine. Whatever. The book was trash anyway."

"You sit your butt right back down." The white woman at the very edge of the semicircle pointed a bony finger in Winnie's direction. She had fiery red hair Winnie assumed came from a box and gold-brown eyes that kind of clashed with it. "If you're going to talk nonsense, you better at least be smart enough to explain yourself."

"She probably didn't read the entire book," the old white man to Winnie's left said, for about the thirtieth time. His posture was perfect—his legs crossed in front of him as he balanced the book on his knee. He had a funny little mustache that was perfectly white, even though the hair on his head was dark gray. "I'm here because you said this would be a serious book discussion. None of this seems very serious to me."

"I'm serious," Winnie said. She was the *most* serious. Her dad's favorite joke was *Winnie doesn't know how to laugh!* though she didn't know why she was supposed to laugh at *that* anyway. Especially when her mom was finally laughing again, and Winnie figured her mom deserved to have all the laughter, and Winnie could save it all for her.

"She belongs to Maude," the fiery redhead said.

"She's helping her daughter and son-in-law out by keeping her for the summer."

"What, are they too busy to take care of her themselves?"

"Is Maude even allowed to do that?"

"I do not *belong* to Maude," Winnie said. "But it *is* true that she is my grandma."

"Did you read the book?" the perfect posture man asked again.

Winnie wanted to kick him in his perfectly straight shins. "I read the book," Winnie said. Again.

"Oh, just let her stay," Jeanne Strong said, patting Winnie's knee. Jeanne Strong was a tall Black woman who lived next door to Winnie's grandma and purposely sat next to Winnie when she saw her. She had a broken wrist enclosed in a neon-pink cast that she refused to let anyone sign. Even though almost everyone in the clubhouse had asked, as if they were the students in Winnie's fifth grade class, who'd had the same excited reaction when Owen Coleman broke his arm last year.

Jeanne and Winnie's grandma did not get along, but they did not get along in that polite way where they said nice things to each other, but really meant *I hope you fall off the face of the earth, please.*

When Winnie's parents had dropped Winnie at her grandma's, Jeanne was the first in the community to come over to greet them. She brought a lasagna. Winnie didn't know what happened to that lasagna, but she knew for certain they never ate it.

Anyway, the hour was half over, and Winnie was having regrets. She'd grabbed the stupid book out of boredom and signed up for the book club to avoid canasta (and her grandma), but this wasn't worth it. Nothing—not being dumped at her grandma's, or her dad's new job, or her mom's returning smiles—seemed completely worth it yet.

Only, Winnie was stubborn enough to at least see this through. "I read the book," Winnie said again, meeting her eyes straight on with Perfect Posture Man. "Did *you?*"

TWO

AS THEY WALKED ACROSS THE STREET TOWARD WHAT WINNIE was supposed to be calling home for now—a little house in a block filled with the exact same little houses, surrounded by a gate that separated the senior citizen community from the road, from the beach, from the ocean Winnie could hear through the windows at night—Winnie's grandma was *not* amused. How she could inject so much disappointment and frustration into the five-minute walk from the clubhouse, Winnie had no idea.

"You need to behave yourself when you're at that clubhouse, Winnifred. We had this talk already."

Winnie didn't even bother defending herself, because really, what was the point? She stuck her hands deep into her jeans pockets, slumped her shoulders, and shuffled her feet—all things she knew her grandma hated. If she'd had her headphones, she would've put them in to drown out both her grandma's lecture *and* the noise of the waves crashing against sand, two sounds Winnie was learning she hated.

"Also, those jeans are sagging right at your butt because you've worn them the entire week. It's too hot for jeans! We had *this* talk already, too!"

Winnie's grandma was in a bad mood. She wasn't always this crabby. She and Winnie actually got along, once. But that was back when they only saw her on Christmas and Easter (and sometimes not even then), back before Winnie's dad decided it would be a good idea for Winnie to spend the summer with her, even though she was Winnie's *mom's* mom and not his.

Both Winnie and her grandma had been pretty moody since Winnie moved in. Winnie was pretty sure her grandma was moody because she loved her family—but from afar. She had her own social life and friends and senior citizen community now. She was done raising kids. She'd also thought she was done raising children before Winnie's mom—oops—came along. But she raised that baby, too, and now here she was again, with a twelve-year-old in her daily care.

And Winnie . . . Winnie was moody because of the things Winnie's parents decided right before they sent her to her grandma's community. She was full of anger she didn't know what to do with.

Winnie's dad said she had nothing to worry about, that she should just enjoy her summer at the shore with her grandmother, but Winnie was actually *more* worried.

Her mom always said, "Your grandma and I never understood each other, so it's easier to be close at a distance."

Yet here Winnie was, living with her grandma.

"I'll make a deal with you," Winnie's grandma said as they walked inside, the cool air from the AC hitting Winnie's face like a snowstorm. Her grandma liked it extra cold.

Winnie kicked off her shoes. "What?"

"You throw away those jeans and I'll tell Carla and Jeanne and the rest of them to shut the hell up about it and let you be in their book club." Winnie's mom was the youngest of six children, so by the time Winnie's grandma had her, she was already pretty old. Which made Winnie's grandma one of the oldest people in the community. Which made her someone the others didn't bother messing with.

"I like these jeans."

"I can see that, but they're starting to smell." Winnie's grandma made her way into the kitchen, where she opened the refrigerator and stared into it.

Winnie weighed her options. "Fine, I'll chuck the jeans. But you make whatshisface stop asking me every five seconds if I've read the book. I'm twelve, I can read."

"Liam Porter. Just ignore him. He's got his own issues."

"Jeanne Strong was nice, though. She was the only one who said I could stay."

"Jeanne Strong doesn't know how to mind her own business. What did I tell you about that?"

"That I shouldn't share our business *inside* the house with anyone *outside* of it," Winnie mumbled, then added more loudly, "Can we order Timoney's pizza for dinner?"

Winnie's grandma sighed. "No. I'm looking at the leftovers."

"We *already* ate the leftovers."

"Guess I'm cooking, then."

"I can make grilled cheese," Winnie said. She didn't like having to rely on her grandma. Because if she had to constantly depend on her instead of her dad and mom, then, well . . . would they ever actually come back for her?

Winnie's grandma nodded. "Fine. But add a tomato so you get some sort of vegetable in there."

Winnie's grandma's place in the senior citizen community had one bedroom. That bedroom belonged to her grandmother.

So, Winnie?

Winnie got the couch.

Her small suitcase was shoved in the corner of the living room, where her clothes were getting wrinkled because she just kept shoving things out of the way when looking for what she wanted to wear each day. Never mind that her grandma said she could have the hall closet and that she could have a drawer in her grandma's dresser, too. Winnie didn't want either. She didn't want space in her grandmother's house. She didn't need a closet or a drawer when she had *both* of those things back home.

She'd continue to sleep on the couch in her old sleeping bag, like a sleepover, which was all this was. Temporary. Her mom or dad could say the word and she would be ready to go home in seconds.

The other good thing about having the couch was that her grandma went into her room to "settle into bed" by eight p.m. every night. She'd disappear to watch her shows, and she never asked Winnie if she wanted to watch with her, which Winnie absolutely did not.

Once her grandma was behind her bedroom door, Winnie took her phone out to FaceTime her mom. Winnie hadn't quite mastered being able to tell if her mom was smiling just by listening to her.

Her mom picked up, her face close to the screen as she yawned right into it. "Winnie, hey," she said. She reached up, stretching. Winnie couldn't see more than her head and neck and the top of her mom's scrubs, but she could picture the scene. She was probably stretching so big her scrubs top lifted up, revealing the belly ring that she really should take out, considering how big she was when Winnie left. She was probably even bigger now, and her stomach had already been widening and pushing her belly ring out, making it look kind of gross.

Oh, right. Winnie's mom was pregnant.

Which wasn't necessarily the reason Winnie had to stay with her grandma for the summer, but wasn't *not* the reason, either.

Winnie's mom groaned and continued stretching. Her hair, pulled up in a haphazard bun, unraveled a little more with the movement. Unlike Winnie's grandma, who was old, Winnie's mom was decidedly young. Sometimes people thought she was Winnie's babysitter, or worse, her big sister—and it stood out especially after Winnie spent an entire day arguing with old people.

"Long day?" Winnie asked.

"Super long," her mom said. "Spent my day with cranky old people."

"Yeah, you and me both." Winnie scowled in her grandma's dark living room, the sound of her grandma's TV mixing with the sound of the ocean coming in from the window behind her.

Her mom cringed, and Winnie didn't know if it was because of *her* or if maybe the baby moved or something. Winnie felt guilty anyway, just in case she'd done something wrong. Winnie was supposed to be more careful.

Sometimes, though, Winnie couldn't help being a little grumpy. She couldn't help but think that a lot of the things swirling around in her gut that made her feel angry and grumbly were her mom's fault.

"You should get some sleep, Winnie. I miss you! Have fun. Don't forget we're going to come visit on Father's Day."

"I don't want to still be here on Father's Day!" Winnie said, because she had to make sure her mom knew.

"I know." Her mom's voice was quiet, and tired. "But it's a nice, fun summer at the beach, right? Just . . . have a nice, fun summer at the beach? Just while you're there, can you please try for me, Winnie?"

Just while you're there.

That's what Winnie's dad had said before they left their apartment to bring her to her grandma's. When Winnie left behind all her rainbow buttons and pins, as well as her own smiles, stored deep in the back of her closet. When Winnie's dad told Winnie that her grandma didn't know Winnie liked girls *and* didn't know about her mom's sad days. And that, for now, while he and her mom "sorted things out," they were going to keep it all a secret. They would only tell her grandma about Winnie's dad losing his job (and getting a new one), and about the new pregnancy, and about how carefully they all needed to be treading water.

Winnie hated water. But nobody had asked what Winnie wanted.

"Let's keep what happens in our house, inside our house," her dad had said. Winnie was hearing that a lot lately. She felt like there were a lot of different houses for secrets to stay trapped in.

Winnie could sacrifice the rainbows and pins and smiles for her mom, so long as her mom took those smiles for herself.

But that didn't mean she had to be happy about any of it.

THREE

WINNIE WAS FOUR THE FIRST TIME SHE KISSED ANOTHER GIRL.
Their preschool teacher didn't scold them. She didn't
tell them kissing other girls wasn't okay. She just told
them kissing wasn't a good school activity (Winnie dis-
agreed) and they should stick to holding hands instead.

So they held hands for two months, until Winnie
decided she wanted to hold hands with a different girl.

She'd just . . . always liked girls. And she never
thought it was something she shouldn't talk about,
especially with her mom, who sat her down when she
was four to say, "I love you no matter what, Winnie,

but let's keep kissing in general to a minimum until you're, like, twenty, okay?"

"But I like kissing."

"So I hear." Her mom had winked. "Just promise me you'll only kiss boys or girls who want to be kissed, okay?"

"*Girls*," Winnie emphasized, even back then. "I'll only kiss girls who want to be kissed."

Winnie's mom laughed, and Winnie didn't know what was so funny, but that was back when her mom laughed a lot and at everything.

All of that was why now, as Winnie sat in the corner of the clubhouse in that uncomfortable folding chair, sulking, and she saw a girl across the clubhouse sitting at the canasta table, it killed her that she couldn't just open her mouth like she would have when she was four and say, "Um, wow, that girl is really pretty."

Because, *wow*, she really was.

In fairness, Winnie noticing the other girl wouldn't be weird at all, since she was the only other person there besides Winnie under sixty—more importantly, she even looked about Winnie's own age. She was Asian, with long dark black hair pulled up into a ponytail. She was wearing a yellow sundress and she wasn't wearing shoes. (Was that even sanitary? Those floors were gross, regardless of the bleach smell. But did it really even matter? She looked adorable.) She was also sitting right next to Winnie's grandma.

Winnie was staring. She knew she was staring, but it was confirmed when Jeanne Strong came over out of nowhere to say, "That's Grace Lai's granddaughter. She visits sometimes."

Grace's granddaughter was laughing at something Winnie's grandma said, throwing her head back for this big-bellied laugh that had her ponytail brushing back and forth against her shoulder blades. "What's Grace Lai's granddaughter's name?"

"Pippa Lai."

Pippa Lai. How completely pretty and modern and nothing like Winnifred Maude Nash.

Winnie loved it.

"Do you want me to introduce you?"

"What?" Winnie asked, startled out of her staring.

"You're fixated," Jeanne said. "It might be nice to have a friend to mope with this summer. That one likes to talk, though, I gotta warn you."

Winnie knew she shouldn't be talking to Jeanne Strong about being fixated on other girls, considering her grandma *and* her dad both warned Winnie to *keep things inside the home*, and Jeanne Strong was outside *both* those homes. "What? No. I'm not fixated. And I'm not moping."

"Okay. Sure." Jeanne shoved a book into Winnie's face before Winnie could open her mouth to argue. "For next month's book club meeting. Don't let Liam scare you off. I think you'll like this one. It was my pick."

"You don't know anything about me," Winnie said, which felt true. No one did. No one outside of their family was allowed to.

Jeanne didn't relent. "Read it and prove me wrong, then. Either way, *I'll* enjoy it."

Winnie took the book and looked at the cover. It was wrapped in plastic with a call number on it—the local library loaned out books for the community's book club, Winnie had learned—and the cover pictured a café with the words FRIED GREEN TOMATOES AT THE WHISTLE STOP CAFÉ written over a yellow background.

At least it didn't look like a romance.

"Read it," Jeanne said again. "And go say hi to Pippa."

With that, Jeanne left to shove copies of the book into the others' hands, causing Liam Porter to say loudly, and rudely, "I thought we were going to discourage the child from being in this book club! Not hand her the book like this is perfectly okay!"

Winnie ignored him and continued to sit in the folding chair, book on her lap, looking at Pippa Lai. Pippa was swinging her bare feet under the card table, absorbed in the game, watching Winnie's grandma take her turn.

Winnie knew she would not be introducing herself to Pippa. Because what if she fumbled over her words, or what if she blushed—and what if her grandma noticed that she *felt* things? What if everyone would just . . . *know*? Winnie had never had to hide so she didn't know *how* to hide. What if just by introducing herself to Pippa, Winnie would cause her grandma to ask her dad and mom if Winnie liked girls? That would *absolutely* make waves with her grandma, which Winnie promised her dad that she wouldn't make at all.

At her parents' house, Winnie could hear everything through the thin walls of her bedroom. She heard every word that flew back and forth between her parents while her dad tried to convince her mom that sending Winnie to stay with her grandma was the best idea.

"We need the help. You and I need to deal with all of this, and someone needs to take care of Winnie while we navigate this pregnancy, because what if—"

"Because what if *what*?" Winnie's mom had snapped in a dark tone that made Winnie's stomach hurt. "I moved out of my mother's house when I did for a reason. Asking her for help is just admitting I was wrong."

"We were kids then. It's different now. And we need to think about what's best for you *and* Winnie."

"My mother is not what's best for Winnie. My mother will hurt Winnie. She'll hurt Winnie's big heart full of love for other little girls. Nick, you remember how she was with me. You remember how she was with *Maria*. She's old and set in her ways and never once tried to understand me."

"We won't survive this, Kit!"

"Keep your voice down—"

"We barely survived as is, and I can't do that again."

"You mean me. I'm not . . . I'm better now. Everything is finally getting so much better. And I'm worried—"

"Let me worry, okay? I'll talk to Winnie. I'll make sure everything is okay. It'll be better for her, I promise. She was *here*, Kit, for all of it, and that's not okay. I don't *want* her here for any of this anymore! Do you?"

"No," her mom had said, voice quiet and small. "I guess I don't want that, either."

When Winnie's dad told her that night that yes, she was spending the summer with Grandma, and yes, he had some rules he'd like her to keep in mind . . . how could she disagree?

Because he was right. Winnie *was* there, for all of it. She *was* there, for every time her mom said she was going to be a big sister, and for all of her mom's sad days that never seemed to end. The sad days that took her mom's smiles and her laughter and everything that made her mom *her mom*.

Winnie didn't want to be sent away.

But what kind of daughter would she be if she didn't try to keep the smiles on her mom's face and do what she could to make sure things could get better—for good this time?

It was best to just sit in the corner right now and pretend she never noticed Pippa at all.

Her mom couldn't FaceTime with her that afternoon, even though Winnie kept track of the days she had off, and when her lunch breaks were, so she knew when she was supposed to be free so that Winnie could check for a smile.

But her mom wasn't feeling well. She was currently napping.

Winnie thought about FaceTiming her dad instead, but his smiles were always big when he spoke to her, whether or not he really wanted to be smiling at all.

Winnie was mad that her mom was napping. She was mad that she wasn't feeling well. She was mad that she was trying to have another baby.

Winnie was three the first time her mom and dad sat her down on the couch in their living room to tell her she was going to be a big sister.

She didn't want to be a big sister anymore. That much she knew. And she found it harder and harder, out of all the things she wasn't supposed to talk about lately, to not talk about *that* particular fact the most.

She didn't want to sit in the living room with her grandma anymore, either.

"You're in a mood again," her grandma said after Winnie loudly sighed for the fifth time. "You call your mom too much as is. Maybe put the phone away for a while. I'll make some calls and set up a playdate."

"I'm not a baby, Grandma," Winnie said. "I don't need you to *set up a playdate.*"

"You need friends. You need to go outside. It's the summer! Go the beach!"

"I hate the beach."

"You do not. No one who lives at the Jersey Shore hates the beach."

"Well, I do."

Her grandma sighed. "Winnifred. Must every conversation be a battle?"

That didn't seem fair. Winnie wasn't the only one battling here. But her grandma was right about one thing: She needed to get outside to just get away from *her.* "Fine. I'm going for a walk, then."

"Good. Don't go far, don't be long, and stay off the seawall," her grandma called after her.

That warning wasn't the only reason Winnie was currently standing on top of the seawall, but it wasn't exactly *not* the reason, either.

Winnie's grandma's senior citizen community was in Sea Bright, New Jersey—which was basically a strip of a town that was surrounded by the Atlantic Ocean on one side and the Shrewsbury River on the other. The seawall was built on the ocean side to protect the town from angry waves and hurricanes. It looked like a big wall made of stones and sand—but that Winnie knew was constructed with concrete and rocks that she could sometimes pry loose—and stretched as far as Winnie could see.

The top of the seawall wasn't entirely smooth, but it was flat enough that you could walk along it, as long as you paid attention. And you had to pay special attention if you were wearing flip-flops. Winnie learned that last year when her flip-flop got stuck between the uneven rocks and she fell down, hard. Winnie—who'd picked at the scab until it wasn't a scab anymore—still had the scar on her knee.

A particularly loud wave crashed against the sand, and Winnie shivered at the sound of it. Despite being a

Jersey girl, Winnie didn't like the ocean. It was almost always cold, and she felt like it was a little too dirty. She also didn't like not being able to see whatever she was stepping on at the bottom.

But the view of the ocean wasn't why she climbed the seawall.

On a clear day, like today, Winnie could *just* make out New York City diagonally across from where she stood, buildings tall and shining with the sun reflecting off them and the water. She had to squint to see it, to make out the shapes of those skyscrapers in the glare, but it was there. She knew it was.

New York City. Where she'd gone on a trip during Christmastime, and there was a man in a bright pink spandex onesie on the subway and no one even batted an eye. Where she watched two boys kiss in a selfie in front of the Rockefeller Center Christmas tree. Where she heard five different languages being spoken before it was even lunchtime, where it seemed like nobody had to hide, nobody's parents were telling them to keep their business inside, where Winnie knew she needed to be.

"Hello!"

Winnie jumped, nearly losing her footing on the wall. She looked down to the beach and saw a girl waving up at her.

Winnie almost lost her balance all over again when she realized the girl was Pippa Lai.

"Don't scare her off, Pippa!" another voice called out, and Winnie noticed a group of kids about her age standing in a clump near the edge of the water. They were all in their bathing suits, letting the waves lap at their feet.

"Pippa will try and make friends with anything!" another voice added. "There isn't even anyone standing up there! It's all a mirage!"

"You've been in the sun too long, Pippa!"

The cackling laughter that followed mixed with the calls of the seagulls that flew a little too close to Winnie's head.

Winnie was about to shout back that she was real, thank you very much, but when she looked back down, Pippa was already walking away, headed toward the group, as if Winnie wasn't actually there at all.

Maybe she really was just a mirage. Everything about her grandma's house felt fake, and temporary, and Winnie didn't want to be here anyway. Winnie wanted to be back in her real house, to her real life, with her real friends and family.

So, fine. Whatever. She shouldn't be talking to Pippa and her pretty face anyway.

She made her way down the other side of the seawall and crossed the street to her grandma's house. On this side of the wall, she couldn't see the beach, or the ocean, or the city on the other side.

Someday, Winnie wouldn't have to squint to see the city. She wouldn't have to search for it across the sea. She wouldn't feel like it was a mirage, floating across the water, beckoning her to something she'd never reach.

She would be part of that city someday.

She would make sure of it.

FOUR

WINNIE WAS GETTING DESPERATE. IT WAS SUMMER BREAK, AND she had nothing to do, and no friends to do that nothing with. If she had to sit at the clubhouse for one more afternoon, she was going to surrender and beg, "Please, Grandma, please set me up on a playdate so I don't need to spend another hour of my life at this stupid clubhouse!" Even though her grandma would never let her hear the end of it.

Which was why, when her mom's best friend, Maria, showed up at Winnie's grandma's door late that morning, way before her grandma was going to drag Winnie to the clubhouse, Winnie nearly cried she was so relieved.

"Hey, Mrs. Nash!" Maria called through the screen door. She lived much closer to Winnie's grandma than Winnie's parents did and had promised she'd visit this summer, though Winnie had completely forgotten. "I thought maybe I'd take Winnie out for lunch."

"You should have called first," Winnie's grandma said. She didn't get up from the couch to let Maria inside, but Maria didn't seem to be deterred. It wasn't really a secret that Winnie's grandma didn't like Maria, who had been best friends with Winnie's mom since middle school.

"It was a last-minute decision." Maria ran her hand over her shaved head, the motion causing her long feather earrings to rock back and forth. She had on a Captain Marvel tank top and black boots (even though it was summer and they were technically at the beach), and Winnie thought she was the coolest person in New Jersey, if not the world.

"Winnie has things to do here," her grandma said. "You can't just spring this on us. She has book club."

"No, I don't," Winnie said. "Book club only meets Fridays. Today is Tuesday."

"You need to read the book, then. Did you even start it?"

Winnie scoffed. "I *will*, Grandma. *After* I have lunch with Maria."

Her grandma waved a hand in the air, going back to watching the TV, and Winnie counted that as both a dismissal and a win. She grabbed her flip-flops and pushed open the screen door to fall right into Maria's arms.

Maria was more like an aunt to Winnie than her actual aunts and uncles, sometimes almost like a big sister who was too old to actually be her big sister, but just as fun. Maria had always been around. She and Winnie's mom rarely went long without seeing each other or talking to each other, and even after Winnie's mom's sad days—when she'd stopped answering Maria's phone calls and started shutting herself in her bedroom any time Maria came over—they picked up right where they left off, no distance between them.

During the hard months, Winnie liked to consider *herself* Maria's best friend. Winnie remembered a conversation Maria and her mom once had after Maria had broken up with one of her ex-girlfriends, where Winnie's mom had said, "Good riddance," and Maria had gotten upset. Her mom explained, "Maria, did you ever actually feel held by Karen? Because I don't think she ever gave a damn."

Winnie liked the idea of that, of making someone feel held. She tried making her mom feel held when she was too sad and tired to leave her bedroom, but her mom didn't want anyone to hold her. So, for the long months when her mom didn't want to be Winnie's mom and didn't want to be Maria's best friend, Winnie focused on making Maria feel held, instead. Maria, for those long months, was the only one who held Winnie right back.

Maria told Winnie she wanted to take her to a nice, fancy lunch place, which meant that she got to ride in Maria's bright blue Civic, with all the windows down and the music on blast for ten entire minutes. They went to a little café in Pier Village where they could sit outside and enjoy the sun, watching the people walking along the boardwalk, listening to the waves against the sand.

"What're you going to get?" Maria asked as she scanned the menu.

"Can I have an iced coffee?" Winnie asked.

Maria gave her a look. "Your mom would probably want me to ask if you'd like an iced tea instead."

"Mom's not here," Winnie pointed out.

Maria didn't argue with that.

When the waitress came to ask what they wanted, Winnie ordered her iced coffee.

"How's your grandma treating you?"

"Dreadful, Maria. You have to come save me more often."

Maria laughed. "You sound just like your mom. I feel like I've just been transported back to middle school, sitting with her in the cafeteria, having the exact same conversation."

"If my grandma's so bad, I don't know why they'd make me spend *all summer* with her."

The waitress returned and put their coffees in front of them, iced for Winnie and hot for Maria, which she always drank no matter the weather. Maria took a sip from her steaming cup and said, "She's not so bad. Not really. Mothers and daughters are complicated sometimes, Winnie. Your mom and your grandma are the poster humans for that."

"What about me and my mom?"

Maria smiled at her. "Your mom is struggling. But I know that you are, too. Try letting yourself just . . . *be*, this summer, Winnie. You're at the beach. Make some friends. Have some fun. Be a kid. You've got a permanent frown on that face lately."

She didn't know what *being at the beach* had to do with anything, but now her dad, *and* Maria, *and* her grandma had used it as a selling point.

"I don't need to smile," Winnie said.

"Okay, well, *I* really need you to find something to smile about while you're here."

Maria stuck the tips of her fingers into Winnie's cold coffee, flicking the droplets into Winnie's face.

"That was gross!" Winnie said, immediately sticking her hand into her drink to flick back at Maria.

"There's that smile!" Maria said.

Winnie hadn't even realized that she *was* smiling. She paused, trying to smooth out her features, trying not to waste a smile on something so silly.

"So," Maria said, her eyes fully on Winnie. "I was thinking maybe you would want to come to Pride in the city at the end of the month with me."

Winnie gasped. "What! Really?"

Winnie *absolutely* wanted to do that.

"Really, really," Maria said.

Winnie had never been to Pride, but she'd seen so much about it on TV and heard so much about it from Maria—about their community, their people. The ones she shared with Maria, but not with her mom or her dad or her grandma. A celebration of people coming together to support one another, to celebrate the love they had for one another. To celebrate love and each other, period.

That, Winnie thought, would be what it felt like to be *held*.

Winnie needed to be in the city. She *needed* to go to Pride. She needed to figure out how to just . . . escape and be *in the city* and be *held*.

She was going to say yes, and she was going to go back and tell her grandma to block it off in her calendar so that she couldn't make a fuss when Maria showed up to take her.

But wait.

Her grandma.

Winnie was staying with her grandma all summer.

Winnie had left all her rainbow pins at home. She had promised her dad she wouldn't say anything to her grandma about being gay.

"That's okay," Winnie quietly said. "Maybe next year?"

"What?" Maria asked. "You gave me the silent treatment for practically an entire week last year because I didn't bring you."

"Yeah, but . . ." Winnie didn't know what to say. She fiddled with her napkin. Did Maria count as bringing the inside-the-home stuff to someone outside of the home? Was Maria part of the family, or was she not supposed to say things to her, either? "It's just . . . I'm with my grandma all summer, so . . ."

Maria waved her off. "I'll call your mom, have her work out the details."

"Well, but . . ." Winnie started, but Maria was already pulling out her cell phone. "Wait, Maria, don't—"

"Kit! Hey! Guess who I'm spending lunch with." Maria winked at Winnie, and then lowered the phone to say to Winnie, "Your mom says hi!" before focusing back on the call. "Hey, so Pride in the city is in a few weeks—can you let your mom know that I'll be taking Winnie? It was a struggle just to free Winnie for lunch today, so I want to go through all the 'proper channels' or whatever so I can take her to Pride."

Winnie couldn't hear what was happening on the other end of the phone.

She didn't need to hear it, though.

She could see the smile on Maria's face slowly disappear.

She could imagine any smile that may have been on her mom's face disappearing, too.

This was exactly why Winnie should never smile. Nothing good ever came from it.

"You're telling me you made the decision to keep Winnie in the closet all summer?" Maria asked, eyes wide, her voice hushed even though Winnie was sitting *right there* and could hear her. "Oh my God, that is so messed up. Winnie has nothing to be ashamed of."

"I know that!"

Winnie *did* hear that. Her mom's voice rose through the phone, and it made Winnie nervous, made Winnie afraid that her mom would shut down and shut everyone out again.

"It's okay," Winnie said, reaching out for Maria, because she needed Maria to drop the subject before she made things bad. "It's okay. I don't want to go. Maybe next year? When I'm not staying with my grandma anymore?"

Maria got really quiet for a moment, her eyes on Winnie. She brought the phone away from her mouth to say something to Winnie but seemed to change her mind. Instead, she brought the phone back to her mouth. "This is so messed up. You know that, right?" Maria said to Winnie's mom. "This is between you and your mom, Kit. *Your* relationship with her. Not Winnie's."

"Maria," Winnie said again. "*Please* stop."

Maria narrowed her eyes and Winnie worried she wouldn't stop. But then she slumped back in her seat and said, "Okay. We'll go next year, Winnie."

Maria said goodbye to Winnie's mom and hung up the phone.

The waitress came back to ask what they wanted to eat, but Winnie wasn't hungry anymore.

Winnie and Maria didn't talk much on the car ride back to Winnie's grandma's house. What was worse, it was only two-thirty, so Winnie would *still* have to be dragged to the clubhouse anyway.

"Sunshine baby," Maria suddenly said.

"What?" Winnie practically barked. She was filled

with the anger and disappointment of not being able to go to Pride, and she didn't know what to do with that anger (she couldn't yell at her mom, she *couldn't*), so it swirled inside her, bouncing around and trying to find a way out.

Maria softly smiled. "I read the other day that a baby born after a miscarriage is called a rainbow baby. Because rainbows come after storms, or whatever."

"Oh," Winnie said, and sunk lower in her seat. *She* was supposed to get the rainbows.

"You were a sunshine baby," Maria said. "The *calm before*. What everyone wants to celebrate and bask in."

Winnie didn't feel all that celebrated, or basked in, or held. Especially since, after everything, this was the very first time anyone had ever said the word *miscarriage* in front of her on purpose.

She barely knew what it meant, had only recently started to piece things together that no one would talk to her about.

"That's stupid."

"It's just something I read," Maria said. "Anyway, you're *our* sunshine, Winnie. You know that, right?

You make me and your mom and dad happy when skies are gray and all that?"

"I know," Winnie said, because it was true. That didn't make any of the anger go away. "But don't call me Sunshine Baby ever again."

When Winnie got out of Maria's car, she shut the door harder than necessary.

Winnie had left her grandma's house that morning in almost a good mood, but she returned to it in a much worse mood than she thought possible. She shoved open the front screen door and didn't bother taking off her flip-flops when she walked inside since her grandma would inevitably be dragging her right back out anyway, like she always did on weekdays.

Winnie paused, confused, when she heard laughter from the kitchen. Especially since the laughter sounded like it came from someone decidedly not old, and who the heck would her grandma have in her kitchen on a weekday afternoon anyway?

She made her way into the kitchen and stopped, mid-step, when she found the source of the laughter.

"Oh, you're home," her grandma said. "And dragging sand into my kitchen, how nice."

Winnie ignored her.

Because standing right next to Winnie's grandma, drinking a big glass of lemonade, was Pippa Lai.

"Hey!" Pippa said as if this were a regular occurrence. "Great, you're home!"

"Great, I'm home," Winnie said, sort of dazed, as she looked desperately at her grandma for some sort of explanation.

"Your grandma asked my grandma if we wanted to set up a playdate, but I didn't want to wait, so I came over to talk your grandma into letting us hang together while she goes to the clubhouse this afternoon! She wasn't sure if you'd be home, which would have been a bummer, but awesome you are, do you have a bathing suit?" Pippa said, all in one breath, as if they were already friends.

Winnie didn't know how to react. "In my suitcase."

"You've got one hour," Winnie's grandma said. "You be back when I'm back, got it?"

"Yes! Promise!" Pippa answered, and then turned to face Winnie. "Come on, get your suit!"

"Where are we go—" Winnie started to say, but any question she may have wanted to ask got trapped on her tongue the moment Pippa reached out and took Winnie's hand.

Because Pippa's hand was soft and lovely in Winnie's.

After she grabbed her bathing suit and they headed out the door, Winnie could only hope her grandma could not tell how hard she was blushing.

FIVE

PIPPA WASN'T ALLOWED ON THE BEACH WITHOUT SUPERVISION, so there Winnie sat at the pool, on a plastic lounge chair that was one of a long line of plastic lounge chairs that encircled the public pool at the Sea Bright Beach Club.

Pools weren't as bad as oceans—at least Winnie could see through the clear, chlorine-heavy water to the bottom—but there were so many people in it that she felt her heart thump a little wildly at the thought of getting in.

"You don't want to swim?" Pippa asked, immediately pulling off her cover-up, revealing a light blue tankini. It didn't matter how hot it was outside, Winnie's face would have been flushed anyway.

But it *was* hot, so Winnie moved from the plastic beach chair (that stuck to her thighs when she got up) to sit on the cement edge of the pool, sticking her feet in the cool water while Pippa swam.

"You should come in, Winnifred," Pippa said, her elbow resting on the concrete side of the pool, her hand touching Winnie's knee.

"Oh, God. It's Winnie. You can just call me Winnie," Winnie said, inching a little closer so the water came farther up her legs. "And I'm fine right here. Really."

"Winnie, then." Pippa's smile was big, and Winnie almost smiled back.

A younger kid jumped in right beside them, and Winnie leaned away from the splash. Pippa didn't seem to mind it, or the fact that the beach club was pretty packed.

"You don't talk much," Pippa observed, before holding her nose and going under the water.

Winnie watched Pippa do a somersault before coming back up for air.

"I do," Winnie said. "I talk plenty. Just, you know, when I feel like it. Or to people I know."

"You know me."

"I just met you."

"Time how long I can hold my breath. I've been working on it."

Pippa dove back under.

Winnie started counting in her head. She looked around the pool at the umbrellas attached to the backs of the lounge chairs, at the line of people at the snack stand, at the crowd of people in the water. It was a bright, sunny day, and Winnie had forgotten to grab sunglasses. It was loud, too, from people chatting and children shouting and laughing and splashing. Even the sounds of flip-flops on puddle-covered cement was noisy.

It was easier when Pippa was underwater. She was blurry and indistinguishable from anyone else in the pool, and Winnie didn't have to worry about the possibility of a crush.

But Pippa wouldn't stay underwater long, and once she came back up, Winnie would have to face those things all while wondering if the heat on the back of her neck was from the sun or the girl looking up at her.

"Oh, no, wait, that's Pippa!"

Winnie turned at the sound of Pippa's name, spotting a group of girls with towels in their hands and sunglasses on their heads. The one in the front of the pack had stopped walking, causing the others to bump into her from behind.

"I cannot handle a dose of Pippa today! We hung out with her all day yesterday—it was too much!"

"Quick! Turn around! Go to the beach instead!" The group immediately did an about-face to leave as quickly as they could. Quick enough that the lifeguard blew his whistle and said, "No running!" as they scurried by him.

A mere second later, Pippa popped her head out of the water. "How long was that?"

Winnie, flustered, had lost count completely. "Uh. Thirty-seven seconds?"

"Oh, shoot! It felt like a lot longer!"

Winnie awkwardly shrugged. She turned back toward where the group of girls was, but they were long gone now. When Winnie glanced down at Pippa, she was doing a somersault underwater. Winnie watched her carefully. What was it about this girl that made an entire group flee so suddenly?

Winnie didn't get a chance to wonder long. Someone suddenly plopped down right next to her. "I can't swim, either."

Winnie startled as she turned to face the girl beside her, whose voice was so soft Winnie wouldn't have heard her if she hadn't practically said it directly into Winnie's ear. She was chubby and wearing an oversized T-shirt with the Rook Coffee blackbird logo pulled over her knees, which were pulled up to her chest, her feet firmly on land. Her hair was thick and wild in a saltwater-messy way, pulled back in a ponytail that wanted to escape from the band she'd wrapped it up in. Her bright orange sunglasses were pushed on top of her head, keeping her hair instead of the sun out of her eyes.

"I can swim," Winnie said. "I'd just rather not."

"Oh," the girl said, and then started to stand back up again.

"My name's Pippa Lai," Pippa loudly said, swimming over to lean between Winnie and the new girl, who sat back down, looking relieved. Pippa made eye contact with Winnie.

"Oh," Winnie said. "I'm Winnie."

"I'm Lucía." She pulled at the neck of her T-shirt. Winnie could see that Lucía was sweating. "Uh, Delgado. Lucía Delgado."

"Why are you at the pool if you don't know how to swim?" Pippa asked in a tone that was much nicer than anything Winnie would have managed.

Lucía pointed over at a group of girls. A skinnier version of her stood among them, hair just as thick and messy but dripping onto the towel she had wrapped around her body. "My sister is on the swim team. She wanted to stay and hang after practice, and my mom wanted me to get some sunshine. My other sisters are on the beach with their own families."

"How many sisters do you have?" Pippa asked.

"Five. I'm the youngest, most of them are a lot older." Lucía motioned toward her sister and her swim team friends again. "Camilla is closest in age to me, but everyone else is already an adult."

It reminded Winnie of her mom and all her mom's much older siblings.

"My mom suggested I make new friends," Pippa suddenly said, avoiding the kicking, splashing feet of a younger kid as he doggy-paddled by. "I chose Winnie, so we came here."

One of the smaller kids swimming along the pool wall grabbed for Winnie's foot to keep themselves steady, and Winnie shrieked, jerking back, startled by the sudden pull on her leg.

Pippa laughed. "He scared you good!"

Lucía softly chuckled, too.

Winnie felt hot as they looked at her, expecting her to laugh or smile with them.

The sun continued to be much too warm.

"I think I've had enough pool time," Winnie said. She pushed against the cement to propel herself to standing. "I should go anyway. I'm going to go. My grandma will be in a mood if I don't get home before she does."

"I'll walk you back." Pippa pressed her hands against the edge of the pool and lifted herself up. Winnie took her hand to help, and Pippa pulled herself to her knees and then stood up beside her. Lucía stayed where she was, looking up at the two of them.

"Maybe I'll see you both again?" Lucía asked.

Winnie didn't know what to say, but Pippa nodded. "I'm visiting all summer."

It made Lucía smile again, bigger this time, and that smile changed Lucía's entire face. It reminded Winnie of how different her mom looked when she was happy, too.

So Winnie found herself saying, "Yeah, we'll be back again soon."

Lucía kept smiling.

Pippa didn't want to walk on the seawall. Winnie wouldn't make her do anything she didn't want to do, but Winnie wanted to walk on the seawall, so she did. Pippa didn't actually hesitate to follow her up there anyway.

Pippa trailed Winnie as she walked along the seawall in the direction of the city, even though they'd already passed the street they needed to turn down to get to Winnie's grandma's house. Winnie was too busy squinting to see the New York skyline across the ocean to care. Pippa didn't seem to mind; she'd found a loose rock and she was kicking it as they walked.

"What're you looking for?" Pippa asked, covering her eyes to block the sun and staring in the same direction as Winnie.

Winnie waved at the skyline. "The city. It's not a great view from here, but you can almost always see it," Winnie said. She was able to see it much better from the boardwalk by her real home.

"Is that where you moved from?" Pippa asked.

"I didn't move. I'm just staying with my grandma for the summer. But anyway, no. I want to move *there* someday, though, maybe. And I want my mom's best friend, Maria, to take me . . ." Winnie drifted off. She couldn't tell Pippa she wanted to go to Pride, because that would open up a can of worms. Pippa could easily open her big mouth and tell Winnie's grandma, and then her grandma would know, and Winnie's mom would get upset. "I want Maria to take me there. To the city."

"I live in Queens. I like it here, though." She stopped walking, and Winnie stopped, too, because she supposed they really should head back around toward home. Pippa tilted her head. "Mostly. I like being at the beach. Sometimes I don't like everyone who is *on* the beach."

Now would be a good time for Winnie to ask Pippa about the girls at the pool, if only she could get her mouth to move. *Who don't you like on the beach, and why don't those girls like hanging out with you?*

Pippa started talking again first. "I've got you here now, though, to look forward to every year!"

Winnie's cheeks were on fire. "Just for this summer."

Pippa's forehead creased. "Oh."

Winnie took another step, and something crunched below her flip-flop. She lifted it up to see what it was.

"Oh!" Pippa said. "Sea glass!"

It was indeed sea glass. Two big pieces, sea-salted and round and deep royal blue. Winnie reached down to pick them both up, and they were soft and smooth as she ran her fingers over them.

"One for each of us," Pippa said.

Winnie placed the larger of the two into Pippa's hand.

"It's fate," Pippa said. "We're friends now. We've got friendship sea glass."

Winnie stared at the sea glass in her hands.

Pippa started walking again, launching into a speech about everything she loved about Sea Bright—from the sand crabs to the seashells to the way the seagulls liked to swoop down and steal sandwiches right out of people's hands—as they climbed down the wall to head home.

Winnie held the sea glass in her fist tightly all the way to her grandma's house.

SIX

AFTER DINNER, WINNIE WRAPPED HERSELF UP IN THE BLANKETS
on the couch that was now her bed, reading the book
that Jeanne Strong had chosen for book club, rubbing
her fingers along the sea glass she still had in her hand.

She was having a hard time focusing. She kept thinking about Pippa, and the pool, and Pride, and Maria,
and her grandma, and how she hadn't FaceTimed her
mom that day. It was all exhausting, really. Which
made the words on the page wobbly and harder to
read. Winnie rubbed her eyes and fought the urge to

just chuck the book across the room. She reached for her cell phone instead.

"I almost forgot to take this out of my pants," her grandma suddenly said, pulling coins and bills out of her pockets and dropping them into the hollow glass turtle she kept on the kitchen counter. She kept her spare change there, and it had been getting really full lately from all the canasta games she'd been winning.

"You should buy us a pizza with that," Winnie said.

"Come play and get better at the game so you can earn your own pizza," her grandma replied.

"It's too confusing!"

"It is not," her grandma said. "Come in here. I'll show you."

Winnie shook her head. "You already showed me, and all I did was lose. Badly. I didn't understand any of it."

"We'll take it one step at a time," her grandma said, grabbing two decks of cards and taking a seat at the table. She gestured to the seat across from her. "Well?"

Winnie put her book down. It wasn't like she was reading it right now anyway. "Okay, fine," she said, crossing the room and sitting at the table. "But this is the last time. If I still think it's a stupid game, you can't ask me to play ever again."

"Deal," her grandma said. "But it's simple. We've got two decks. The main object of the game is to outscore the opposing team, or players. Points are scored by forming melds, which are combinations of three or more cards of the same rank, with or without the help of wild cards."

Winnie slunk back in her seat. "This is hopeless."

Her grandma smiled. She actually *smiled*. "Don't be so dramatic. Here, listen."

Winnie groaned.

But Winnie did listen.

And before she knew it, she and her grandma had been playing canasta for an entire hour.

She still didn't really understand or know what to do without her grandma's help (or bossiness) telling her what she needed to do. She was pretty sure it was cheating to say she won when she realized she'd made the most number of melds during their last game together. But, still, she shouted: "I won! Look!"

Her grandma laughed. "See? *Anyone* can win."

"What's that supposed to mean?" Winnie asked.

Her grandma laughed harder.

"Fine. You have a point. I don't think I'm ever going to win us pizza money."

"Well, maybe you earned a pizza for dinner anyway," her grandma said.

Winnie lit up. "Really?" she said. She felt the smile on her face and took a moment to breathe it away.

"Really," her grandma said, and pointed at the designated junk drawer in her kitchen. "There's a menu in there. We'll order now so it gets here before we're starving."

Winnie jumped up to quickly grab the menu.

Her grandma took it from her. "Remind me to make a bunch of premade freezer meals for when your mom has the baby, lest you survive on pizza for the weeks afterward."

Winnie froze at the mention of the baby.

Her grandma, who was mid-dial of the pizza number, froze, too. But then she shook her head and finished dialing, pressing the phone to her ear.

After she ordered, she glanced back at Winnie. Winnie wasn't even close to smiling anymore. She refused to meet her grandma's gaze and she found herself quietly saying, "It was stupid for my mom and dad to do this again."

It was the most Winnie had admitted out loud about her mom's new pregnancy since they'd told her about it.

Her grandma didn't say anything, which made Winnie look up at her, because she was sort of expecting her to scold Winnie for talking about something she wasn't supposed to talk about, not out of the house or in it.

Her grandma wasn't smiling anymore, either. She took a deep breath and leaned over, patting Winnie's leg under the table. "Go finish reading your book club book. The pizza will be here in twenty minutes."

Winnie stayed up all night reading that book.

That wasn't true. She finished a little after one in the morning but stayed up the rest of the night in absolute shock that an older woman—her grandma's neighbor—chose this book. That an entire group of senior citizens was going to be discussing it.

In the same room where her grandma would be playing cards.

(Did everyone else already know this book was gay? Did her grandma? Winnie was so nervous that she slept with it under her pillow so that her grandma wouldn't notice in the morning and ask her about it.)

Look, it wasn't that the book was gay—though it was, it *was!*—but that Winnie didn't know how to . . . not talk about that. Which, she couldn't, right? Even though it was a book club, and two of the main characters, Idgie and Ruth, were *in love*, and the point of a book club was to talk about these things . . . she just couldn't. Right?

Right. Because her grandma would be there, and she lived next door to Jeanne Strong, and she had eyes and ears all over that community, and this would most certainly be bringing inside-the-home things outside of it.

But still, Winnie didn't know how to *not* talk about it.

Winnie was the youngest member of her school's GSA—Gender and Sexuality Alliance. It was her mom who told Winnie about it before the last school year.

"Did you know," her mom had said while Winnie ate her cereal, still half asleep, "your school, I mean, all the schools, at least in Jersey, if any of you guys ask for one of those LGBTQ clubs, they have to make it happen. Like, it's a rule."

"Cool," Winnie had said.

"I checked, though. Your school has one." Her mom passed Winnie more cereal. "In case you were interested."

Winnie felt held then, before her mom lost her smiles again and stopped asking Winnie about the GSA meetings or about girls or about anything.

Winnie didn't want to think about that. She didn't like thinking about how, instead of talking to her mom about her feelings, she was sitting in an uncomfortable folding chair surrounded by Jeanne Strong and Carla and Liam as they began the book club discussion. Winnie made it a point to keep her mouth shut.

Liam was quick to notice. "I bet she didn't read it."

Winnie rolled her eyes.

"Why don't you tell us what you liked about it?" Jeanne asked.

Winnie was saved from answering when Carla butted in: "I'm not entirely sure this was an appropriate book for a ten-year-old." Winnie didn't bother correcting her on her age. "We should have run this by Maude first."

"It's an adult book club," Liam chimed in. "Maude knows we aren't sitting over here reading Dr. Seuss."

"What exactly did you find so inappropriate?" Jeanne Strong asked, and Winnie slumped in her seat because she could tell this was going to become a Thing.

Winnie glanced over to check if her grandma was (hopefully) fully engaged in canasta.

Thank God she was.

But Pippa was sitting there, too, waving right at Winnie, and, well, this would have been a good time to suddenly become invisible, really.

Winnie waved back, though, and Pippa smiled, and Winnie's cheeks turned warm.

"I just think there are certain things Winnie doesn't need to be reading about," Carla said.

"What things?" Jeanne asked, leaning forward, in a tone that Winnie's grandma was fond of using herself. The kind of tone that set a person up to dig themselves a hole. "The issues about race or the queer content?"

"What?" Liam exclaimed. "What queer content?"

"Did you think they were just gal pals?" Jeanne said, raising her eyebrows.

"They were just . . . they were gay?" Liam was practically shouting.

Winnie was dying. He was being so loud. She glanced back at her grandma and Pippa and felt her face flush hotter.

"What did you think of the book, Winnie?" Jeanne asked, ignoring Liam.

Winnie felt too hot. They were all looking at her, and she was supposed to tell them what she thought about this book that she loved—she did, she *loved* it— but how could she explain to them why? How could she tell them Idgie was her favorite because Idgie was strong and tomboyish and stubborn and in love? How could Winnie explain she loved those things because she understood Idgie, and she loved Idgie and Ruth because they were perfect together? They held each other, and Winnie wanted to be held by them, too, but how could she explain any of that without explaining her feelings for girls or about her mom or about all the things she wasn't supposed to be talking about to anyone who wasn't family, even though her family never talked about any of it, either?

Her grandma was ten feet away and she couldn't say how she really felt, so Winnie found herself lying instead. "It was long and dumb and boring."

"See?" Liam said. "She definitely didn't even read it."

Winnie decided right then she was quitting book club.

The hour wasn't over, but Winnie was done. She left the clubhouse, walking into the humid air outside, and pulled out her cell phone to call Maria.

It rang only once before she answered, because Maria always took Winnie's calls. "Hey, you, what's up?"

Idgie and Ruth were gay and in love and I want to tell you about them, Winnie wanted to say. But the words got trapped in her throat. She glanced over her shoulder to double-check that the clubhouse door was closed.

"Winnie?"

She couldn't get her mouth to move, and there was a lump in her throat that made her feel like even if she *could* find the words, she would start crying into the phone instead. She didn't want to cry. She didn't want Maria to hang up, either.

"I wanted to tell you . . ." was the only thing Winnie could say before her throat closed up, and she held her breath to keep the tears that burned her eyes at bay.

The door behind her suddenly opened. Winnie checked the clock on her cell phone. Her grandma was always one of the last people to leave, but still. It wasn't like Winnie could have this conversation while anyone in her grandma's community walked past her.

"Winnie? You still there?"

Winnie moved as far to the side as she could, away from the commotion, and took a deep, shuddering breath. "I'm here."

"What's wrong, Sunshine?"

Sunshine. Winnie was a sunshine baby. Her parents should have been holding on to her so tight because she was *right there*, but they weren't. She wanted Maria to hold her. She wanted her mom to hold her. She wanted someone to tell her this baby would be okay, and her mom would keep smiling and be the one to tell Winnie's grandma, *Winnie likes girls, and we're going to go to Pride to support her.*

"You know, Winnie, I've actually got a surprise for you, if you're up for it," Maria said. "You want to spend a day with me this weekend? It's Asbury Park's Pride Day on Saturday. I know it's not the same as the glamour of the city, but I think you'll really enjoy it."

That lump was back in Winnie's throat. Asbury Park was a couple towns over from theirs, a nice town on a boardwalk, where people were going to come together and celebrate Pride, and she wanted to go. She *did*. But also . . . "I can't. *I can't.*" Her voice was cracking.

"We don't need to tell anyone," Maria said, which was shocking to Winnie. Maria never kept secrets from Winnie's mom. They were best friends. "We can say we're spending the day together on the boardwalk. That's all. Okay? You let me worry about the rest. We're just going to the boardwalk for lunch together Saturday."

You want us to lie? Winnie thought, but couldn't bring herself to say.

Because lying actually sounded pretty good right now. Her dad didn't have to know she was bringing inside things to the outside. Her mom didn't have to stress. "Okay," Winnie said.

"Okay," Maria repeated. "I'll pick you up Saturday for lunch, then."

Winnie hung up the phone and had the sudden and intense urge to throw it. She wanted to punch the brick wall of the clubhouse or stomp her feet like a little girl, and she couldn't really explain why. She couldn't do any of that. So instead, she bottled it all up, feeling a knot form in her chest.

"Are you okay?" Pippa was suddenly beside her. "You look like you're going to—"

"I'm fine," Winnie said, clenching her jaw.

"Oh, okay. I mean, if you're not, I'm here if you want to talk about it?" Pippa said, but Winnie didn't waver, because Pippa was being nosy like Jeanne Strong was nosy, and Winnie's grandma would not approve.

Pippa nodded anyway, as if Winnie had responded. "Okay. Do you want to come with me to the movie this weekend?"

Winnie blinked at her. "What?"

"The movie. On the beach. They show one once a month throughout the summer," Pippa explained. "It's Saturday this month. I was thinking we should invite Lucía, too. Maybe you could invite her? I usually go with . . . well, it doesn't matter who I usually go with."

"The girl from the pool?"

"No, I don't usually go with the girl from the pool."

Winnie shook her head. "No, I mean, you want to invite the girl from the pool?"

Pippa smiled. "Yeah! Lucía! You should invite her. So can you? Come to the movie and invite Lucía?"

"Why can't you invite her?"

Pippa's smile left her face, and Winnie felt bad, because Pippa had a really pretty smile and Winnie didn't mean to scare it off. "She'll say yes if you ask her. My mom thinks I 'come on too strong.'"

"You asked me, though."

"Are you going to come?"

"I might have plans," Winnie said, and Pippa suddenly looked so much smaller, her shoulders slumping and her smile entirely wiped away. It made Winnie backtrack almost immediately. "But the plans are during the day? So I might be able to go after I get home, if it's early enough. Is that okay?"

"That's great!" Pippa said, and then wrapped her arms around Winnie in a hug. Winnie felt her entire body tense up, and the back of her neck and her cheeks grew warm, and she barely had time to hug Pippa back before she was letting go.

Winnie couldn't help but smile.

And then Pippa was smiling again, too.

Maybe it was okay to share *one* of her smiles with Pippa.

"See you later, Winnie! Don't forget to invite Lucía!"

Winnie's grandma came out of the clubhouse as Winnie watched Pippa leave. Her grandma bumped a shoulder into Winnie's. "Ready to go? I think you've been in the sun a little long. You look a bit sunburned."

Which only made Winnie turn redder.

SEVEN

MARIA KEPT HER WORD AND TOLD WINNIE'S MOM—WHO TOLD Winnie's grandma—she was taking Winnie out for lunch, shopping, and fun on the boardwalk. It wasn't a total lie. Maria just didn't mention that the boardwalk they were going to was in Asbury Park, and definitely didn't mention that today was their Pride Day.

Winnie tried not to worry about that almost-lie, tried to let Maria worry about it like she said she would.

Maria waited until Winnie was in the car before she grabbed a bag from the back seat and pulled out two matching rainbow tank tops. She also had makeup in the glove compartment, which she used to decorate Winnie's eyelashes and eyelids in rainbow colors after they had parked the car near the event. She also drew a smiling sun on one of Winnie's cheeks, which Winnie didn't love, but overall she felt excited, happy, held, and closer to *herself* for the first time that summer.

"Ready?" Maria asked.

Winnie smiled. She couldn't help it. She really, really was. "Yeah."

The Convention Hall in Asbury Park was a big building, an indoor exhibition center that connected the Paramount Theatre and the Grand Arcade on either side of the boardwalk, with a green lawn on one side of it, and the beach right behind it. Normally, Winnie would be able to hear the ocean crashing against the sand from where they sat on that lawn, but today the whole town felt like it was packed with thousands of people and families in bright rainbow colors, waving bright rainbow flags, and it was much too loud to hear anything except the buzz of excitement.

There were towels and chairs placed under umbrellas to shade people from the heat of the sun, which was shining brightly in the sky with barely any clouds in sight. Maria and Winnie each had a tailgating chair strapped to their shoulders as they looked for the perfect spot. "We'll sit here to watch the parade come around," Maria said. "And we can mingle, and then get food, and do whatever you want. Sound good?"

Winnie, for once, could not stop smiling. Maria smiled in response, and Winnie let herself have that because she was at Pride and she could not help herself.

"More than good."

And it *was* more than good. It was great. Maria immediately spotted people she knew and pointed Winnie in their direction. "Hey, wait, let's go by Janice and Jake."

Janice and Jake each had a baby hiked up on a hip, and two other kids a little younger than Winnie sat in chairs in front of them, a cooler between them. "Maria! Hey!" the one with short bright pink hair said, handing the baby over and pulling Maria into a hug. "Who've you got here?"

"This is my goddaughter, Winnie." Maria squeezed her shoulders. "Winnie, this is my friend Janice, and that's her partner, Jake." Jake's hair was longer and was blue on the ends. One of the kids in the chairs had matching blue tips. "This is Winnie's first Pride."

"Awesome!" Jake exclaimed, tickling the stomach of the baby they were holding. "It's Lila's first, too!"

"We come every year," one of their kids said.

"Offer Winnie a drink," Janice said. "And Maria, we've got adult beverages, too. Help yourselves."

Winnie took a soda can from their cooler and sat in one of the chairs she and Maria had now placed next to Jake and Janice and their family. Maria and Janice were having a conversation, Jake was fussing with the babies, and the other two kids were playing games on their tablets. Winnie couldn't help but watch them: this family with their sparkles and colorful hair and cheerful faces and willingness to take their kids to Pride every year. Winnie wondered if they went to the one in New York City, too. She wondered if any of the kids were queer, too. She wondered what it would have been like to have a bunch of siblings and parents happy to take all of them to support Winnie and celebrate who she was.

Suddenly the crowd started cheering, and Winnie jumped. Maria leaned over and said, "The parade is coming!"

Winnie stood up so she could see better, but she couldn't see much over the people in front of her. That was okay, though, because the people in front of her—and the people all around her—were a burst of colors and signs and excitement. Someone nearby started chanting, "We love our LGBTQ!" and others joined in, and then everyone joined in, including Maria, who bumped her hip against Winnie with a smile and a wink that made Winnie join in, too.

As the parade made its way down the street, Winnie heard a marching band coming closer. She could just make out the tops of their heads in their matching hats, and she could see a banner that read A STATE OF EQUALITY front and center. People around her started dancing, Jake and Janice lifted their kids up in the air, and Maria took Winnie's hand and spun her again and again until Winnie was nearly laughing.

She felt held. They were partying in the daylight, everyone holding on to everyone else.

And that realization hit her.

Winnie looked around at the other families—like Janice and Jake—embracing their friends and families. She saw kids her age and younger decorated in rainbows, dressed in gender-nonconforming clothes, being themselves and knowing they'd get to go home and continue to do so inside or outside or wherever . . . it made Winnie's stomach hurt.

She'd had to have her mom's best friend lie so she could be here. She'd need to wash the makeup off her face before she got home.

Jake asked if Winnie wanted a rainbow bracelet, like the one she used to have that she'd left behind, and Winnie shook her head no, because she wouldn't be able to wear it at her grandma's house.

She turned around to find Maria again, wanting to maybe have Maria wrap her arms back around Winnie, and that was when Winnie saw her: Jeanne Strong.

Jeanne "doesn't mind her own business" Strong. She was so close Winnie could reach out and touch her.

And she was waving right at Winnie.

The parade was ending, and the party had barely begun, but Winnie looked at Maria, grabbed her arm, and pulled her close to say, "We need to go. I want to go home now."

EIGHT

WINNIE REFUSED TO TALK TO MARIA ON THE CAR RIDE HOME. She couldn't. She searched through Maria's glove compartment and found some Dunkin' Donuts napkins to wipe her face, smearing her makeup all over.

Her face was a mess when they pulled up to her grandma's house, but Winnie figured she could come up with another dumb lie to explain the smudged makeup. She opened the car door and started to climb out.

"Wait, Winnie, hold up," Maria called after her. Winnie paused and turned to Maria, who took a napkin and gently rubbed at the makeup on Winnie's cheeks. "I know you're upset, but if your mom finds out, I'll take the heat, okay? There's nothing to worry about. You're more important to me than a potential fight with your mom."

"You don't know anything," Winnie said.

"I was in the closet until my mid-twenties, Winnie. I think I know a bit more than you're giving me credit for," Maria said.

Winnie sunk in her seat. It was true. Maria had lived with them for a while when Winnie was a baby. She was in all of their holiday photos and at all of Winnie's earliest birthdays. Winnie had asked about it, once. Her mom told her that Maria's family wasn't acting much like family, so they made themselves Maria's family instead. They were the ones to hold her.

But what did that matter when Jeanne Strong could be telling Winnie's grandma, and that would make Winnie's grandma upset, which would make her *mom* upset, and what would happen if her mom got upset again? "You don't know anything!" Winnie said again, and then climbed out of the car and slammed the door.

Winnie wanted to be left alone, but unfortunately, she didn't have a bedroom to hide in (or a bedroom door to slam), and throwing herself face-first onto the couch wasn't as satisfying. She did it anyway.

Her grandma wasn't pleased. "What's your problem?"

"Nothing. I'm just tired. *God*."

"This never-ending mood of yours needs to sort itself out." Her grandma reached over to push Winnie's legs, forcing her into a sitting position. "Jeanne said you flaked out on book club, too."

Great. Jeanne Strong was *already* talking about her. "I didn't flake. It was just stupid."

"Everything to you is stupid lately."

"Can't I just be in a bad mood? Can that just be allowed?"

"Or," her grandma countered, and Winnie pushed her face into her pillow out of frustration, "you could tell me what's wrong, and I can help you find a solution. Just talk to me, Winnifred, instead of growling in my direction."

Winnie didn't respond. She certainly didn't *growl*.

"At the very least, you can help me figure out what to have for dinner," her grandma continued, and Winnie really, really wished she had a bedroom. Or a closet. Or anything to be able to just . . . shut the door and keep her grandma on the outside.

Winnie suddenly felt like she was going to cry, and she did not want to cry in front of her grandma. Especially when she couldn't say what she needed to.

She shoved her hands under her pillow, the better to smoosh her face into it, and felt something smooth and hard underneath.

The friendship sea glass.

"Grandma?" Winnie picked her head up off the pillow, sea glass in her hand. "If I thought of a solution, will you help me?"

Her grandma continued looking through her kitchen cabinets, surveilling them for dinner. "I already told you, Winnie. All you have to do is ask."

"Pippa Lai invited me to see the movie on the beach tonight. Can I go? Can you call Pippa's mom and tell her I want to go?" Winnie asked, and then remembered that Pippa told her to invite Lucía, and Winnie definitely forgot all about Lucía. The problem was, she didn't know anything about Lucía, least of all Lucía's phone number. "And there was a girl at the beach club, I want to invite her, too. Her name's Lucía and she has, like, five sisters, and I think her last name was . . . something with a D."

"I can call Grace Lai," Winnie's grandma said. "I might need more to go on than 'Lucía something with a D.'"

"But you know everyone," Winnie said. "And you said all I had to do was ask."

Her grandma sighed as she picked up the phone. "Let me see what I can do."

Winnie's grandma played phone train for about twenty minutes before she got ahold of Lucía's grandmother Mrs. Delgado, but she *did* get ahold of Mrs. Delgado. When she phoned the Lais' number, Pippa, as expected, shouted into the phone so loudly, Winnie's grandma had to hold it away from her ear. Pippa was even loud enough for Winnie to hear her say, "I didn't think you were going to call! We'll come get you on our way!"

So there Winnie was, with Lucía and Pippa, on the beach for movie night.

It was a different sort of crowded at the Sea Bright

beach that night than it had been at the Asbury Park Convention Center, a different kind of buzz, an overall different kind of feeling. It wasn't even all that loud, though no one was necessarily quiet. Everyone just laid out their blankets or their beach chairs, took out their snacks and drinks, and sat on the sand with their friends and families, all eyes looking up toward the big projection screen.

Pippa's mom had Pippa's two younger siblings far enough away that they had some privacy, but close enough that they couldn't get kidnapped or drown or any of the other things Pippa's mom was worried about. Both Pippa and Lucía brought towels to sit on. Lucía's was big enough to share, and so Winnie did.

Pippa's mom was thrilled about all of it. She greeted them with the world's biggest smile and gave Pippa the world's most obvious wink. "She's happy I made new friends," Pippa explained. Winnie felt a tug in her chest at how easily Pippa's mom kept sending smiles in their direction.

Lucía was digging a hole with her foot as she leaned back on her towel. "She seems nice."

"She is," Pippa said. "What's your family like?"

"Loud," Lucía said, cringing.

Winnie wanted to tune them out as they continued talking about their lives. She wanted to lie back and ignore them and watch whatever Disney movie was inevitably being screened that night and try not to think about her mom, or the baby, or her grandma, or Jeanne Strong or Maria or Pride.

But there was something about Lucía's laugh, quiet as it was—more breath than actual noise—that made Winnie smile without realizing. And there was something about the way Pippa seemed to take every moment of silence as a challenge to find something new to talk about. It all kept Winnie from being able to completely tune out.

Across from them, four sets of towels away, a group of girls—the ones who were at the pool club—and some boys, too, were shrieking and laughing with one another. Winnie watched Pippa glance over at them and then quickly look away.

Winnie couldn't help but ask, "Do you know them?"

Pippa grew quiet, and Winnie worried for a moment that just by being there, she was somehow stealing away Pippa's smiles, too.

"They're my friends who I usually come with.

But . . . last year, it didn't go so good? I thought we were having fun. I made them laugh. We laughed a lot. But the next day they told me I talked too much and ruined the movie," Pippa said.

Winnie turned to glare at the group of them. They didn't sound much like friends.

"They live here all year round and I only come for the summer," Pippa continued. "It's hard to fit in. I try, but they get to be close all school year, so it's hard."

Winnie thought about how they acted at the pool. She didn't think it had anything to do with the fact that Pippa was only here for the summer, and everything to do with the fact that they were being mean.

"Lucía!"

The three of them all turned their heads in the other direction to see Lucía's sister waving at them. Lucía waved back.

"That's my sister and her friends," Lucía clarified. "They always invite me, but I usually say no. This is my first time coming to the movie."

"Why don't you ever go with them?" Pippa asked.

Lucía shrugged. "I don't like hanging out with my sister and her friends. They're all so . . . pretty, and fun, and they swim so good, and their bathing suits are always so cute." Lucía wrapped her arms tightly around her. "My mom says I should try to be more like Camilla. I'm no good at it, though."

"No good at what?" Pippa asked.

"Being pretty and fun," Lucía said, her shoulders creeping up toward her ears as she wrapped herself even more tightly in her own arms.

"We're having fun!" Pippa said, sounding almost offended.

"I think you're pretty," Winnie said before she realized she'd spoken. She felt her face flush immediately. She meant it, though. Lucía wasn't skinny like her sister, and her cheeks were round and looked soft, and her eyes were big and brown, and her eyelashes were so long, and she had this little dimple in her chin that Winnie liked.

Lucía blinked quickly, and Winnie wanted to look away and pretend she didn't see how wet Lucía's eyes were, but she couldn't help but watch those long eyelashes as they fanned against Lucía's brown skin.

Winnie was staring, she realized, and she needed to stop.

She also suddenly realized she wanted to—no, she *needed* to—say something real for once, too. Her face was on fire, but she didn't want to worry about what that meant.

Because she could not shake the way she'd felt at Asbury's Pride, when she was so close to feeling held, but that feeling had been yanked away so quickly.

"I like girls," Winnie said from where she was lying on Lucía's towel, between Lucía and Pippa. They both turned away from the black screen in front of them and looked at Winnie. "I'm gay. I always have been. And I need someone in this stupid town to know it."

The movie started, the projector going bright. Winnie squinted as the hush traveled throughout the beach and the music for the opening credits began playing.

Winnie turned to Pippa. "My grandma doesn't know. Don't say anything."

"I wouldn't," Pippa said, reaching a hand to hold Winnie's. Winnie almost pulled away, but Pippa held tight. "You can trust me."

"Yeah," Lucía said, sitting up and looking at Winnie with her big brown eyes. "Me too."

They all turned their attention to the movie, one that Winnie was sure they'd all seen a million times before. There was a cool breeze that had Pippa zipping up her sweatshirt, and Winnie, now chilled, realized she had been sweating. Telling Pippa and Lucía that she liked girls was scary. It had made her nervous, even a little embarrassed.

She didn't like that feeling.

What she did like was Pippa's hand still wrapped tightly around Winnie's, and how warm Lucia's fingers were as they wrapped around Winnie's other hand. None of them let go as they quietly lay together, watching the movie.

NINE

THE FOLLOWING MONDAY, WINNIE DIDN'T HAVE TIME TO HEAD to her uncomfortable folding chair in the corner of the clubhouse to mope. The moment she and her grandma stepped through the doors into the fluorescent lighting and the smell of peppermint and bleach, Pippa grabbed Winnie's hand and tugged her toward the canasta table.

Her grandma was close behind her, and Winnie was already sitting down at the round table before she could even utter a protest. A tall man with a scruffy face and an Italian accent said, "The more the merrier!" and began shuffling the deck of cards in his hands. Beside him was an older woman—Pippa's grandma, Grace Lai, who looked exactly like a much older Pippa.

She winked at Winnie. "More competition!" she said. "I will not go easy on you!"

Pippa sat sandwiched between Grace and Winnie, and Winnie's grandma sat on the other side of Winnie. Next to her was Carla from book club, followed by a small, frail-looking woman whose hands were shaking as she picked up her cards. Winnie was worried she would shake right out of her seat, but no one else at the table seemed concerned.

"I'm Dom!" the Italian man said. "I have the pleasure of playing with all these beautiful ladies!"

The frail shaking lady blushed. Winnie's grandma and Carla both rolled their eyes.

"Behave," Winnie's grandma said, which sent Dom off into hysterics.

Winnie didn't know which she preferred less: Dom's flirting or Liam Porter's surliness.

Her grandmother slid a crinkled dollar bill over to Winnie. "This is all you get from me," her grandma said. "So play wisely."

Winnie scoffed. "That's it? I'm going to be out after the first round!"

Pippa shifted her seat closer to Winnie, putting her three dollar bills on top of hers. "Here," Pippa said. "We can pool our resources and play together. I'm getting pretty good!"

"No teams!" Carla said.

"Leave them alone," Grace replied.

Winnie's grandma merely fixed Carla with a *look*.

Pippa and Winnie played as a team.

Pippa wasn't any better at explaining how to play the game to Winnie than her grandma was, but at least Pippa did seem to know what she was doing. They lost the first round to Dom, and the second to Grace, but somehow they managed—Pippa managed—to actually pull things together in the third round to win. "Yes!" Pippa exclaimed, leaning forward to collect all the dollar bills and coins in front of her and Winnie.

"Do it again," Winnie said, mostly because Carla *and* Dom were both frowning at them. "Come on, let's do it again."

Both Winnie's and Pippa's grandmas sat the next round out, leaning over their granddaughters' shoulders to see the cards in their hands. They weren't exactly quiet about their support and guidance, which made Carla exclaim, "I said no teams!" sending the frail-looking woman into laughter that shook her entire body.

"Hannah is laughing so hard she's going to have a stroke!" Dom said, chuckling to himself as he quickly took his turn.

"This is the most fun I've had in years," Hannah replied, her voice as trembly as the rest of her. "I love seeing everyone get so worked up!"

"You're such an instigator," Carla said, throwing her hands in the air.

"It's always the quiet ones," Grace replied. "Pay attention, Pippa, you have a meld!"

"I do?"

"Here, because the two is wild," Winnie said, taking their turn.

"That's my girl," Winnie's grandma said close to Winnie's ear, and it made Winnie smile. It made Winnie smile to see Pippa light up in delight as they won—again—and it made Winnie laugh when Dom pretended to be mad and threw all of his cards up into the air. She laughed even harder when Hannah wiped her eyes with a shaking hand because she was chuckling so hard she had tears, and Winnie did not stop laughing when Carla stood up, rolled her eyes, and said, "Your children are taking over *all* my fun these days," even though she was smiling, too. "First book club, now this!"

"I want to join book club!" Pippa said.

Carla held up her hands and walked away from the card table.

Pippa counted the dollars and coins in front of them, separating them into two even piles. Winnie reached out a hand to stop her. "You earned it all. I barely did anything."

Pippa shook her head. "We were a team. You did plenty. Take your winnings, Winnie."

Winnie took the money, crumpling it up and shoving it into her pockets. When she turned to look over at her grandma, she found her looking back at her, smiling. Winnie narrowed her eyes. "What?"

"Nothing," her grandma said in a way that Winnie knew did not mean nothing. "I just haven't seen you have this much fun since you got here. I guess canasta isn't the worst game ever after all, is it?"

Winnie glared at her. She still didn't understand it. And she was still absolutely not any good at it. But, fine. Maybe canasta wasn't *so* terrible.

Her grandma reached for her shoulder, giving her a gentle squeeze and shaking it a bit, making Winnie completely powerless to keep the smile off her face, too.

Winnie was in such a good mood, she didn't even complain when her grandma told her they had to go grocery shopping immediately after leaving the clubhouse, even though Winnie found grocery shopping the worst thing ever, even more so than canasta. But her grandma was determined to not order pizza every time Winnie asked, so they had to get food if they were going to eat.

Winnie's mom usually roamed the aisles aimlessly, deciding what she wanted to make for dinner or eat for lunch while she browsed the shelves—which often meant they had to run back out for milk or eggs or something else they needed. Winnie's grandma, however, had a list a mile long and entered the grocery store like a soldier on a mission. She barked orders at Winnie once they stepped through the automatic doors into the cool air. She rattled off a small list of things she wanted Winnie to grab from one direction, and she headed in another. Winnie didn't like grocery shopping and she certainly didn't like being bossed around, but she had to admit she *did* like how her grandma's efficiency made the trip a lot shorter than it ever took with Winnie's mom.

Winnie's grandma reached for the cart, while Winnie grabbed a handbasket.

Winnie was in charge of the canned tomatoes, the olives, the cans of tuna fish ("The ones in *water*, Winnifred. Do not get the canned tuna in oil!"), and the boxes of pasta. She was told to pick out what cereal she wanted for breakfast. ("None of that sugary cereal. Or those ones with the marshmallows—what're they called?"

"Lucky Charms."

"No Lucky Charms!"

"I don't like marshmallows anyway!")

Winnie stared at the different kinds of Cheerios for about ten entire minutes before she decided to go with something normal, Honey Nut, and threw it into her handbasket along with the tuna she had already gotten, which was indeed the tuna in water. She'd even double-checked—though she knew how to read, despite what Liam Porter might think—before putting it into her basket.

She was looking for the pasta aisle when she turned the corner and found herself in the baby aisle instead.

She looked up at the signs. Pasta was two rows over.

She decided to cut through the baby aisle anyway.

She walked past the shelves of canned baby foods, pureed in glass jars. She read all the flavors: banana, and banana blueberry, and carrot, and—*gross*—turkey and gravy. There were various kinds of apple: apple zucchini peach and apple spinach kale and apple prune. She reached to take one of the glass jars, her face scrunching in disgust as she read *Pear Carrot Pea*, wondering if she ate something this nasty-sounding once, wondering if her mom would feed the baby something this nasty-sounding, too.

With that thought in her head, Winnie quickly put the jar back and took a step away from it.

She started breathing a little heavily, struggling a bit to catch her breath.

"Winnie?"

Winnie startled and turned at the sound of Lucía's

voice. Lucía stood at the end of the aisle holding a box of Cheerios identical to the one in Winnie's basket.

"Hi," Lucía said.

"Hi," Winnie replied.

They stood there in silence for a moment, Lucía shifting her weight from one foot to the other and back again. Usually Pippa was there to fill the gaps in the conversations.

Lucía looked up at the wall of disgusting-flavored baby food. "Oh. Do you have a baby? I mean, not you, obviously, but . . ." Lucía nervously wrung her hands, cringing a bit. "Just, that's baby food, so . . ."

"My mom's having a baby."

Winnie didn't know why she said it. She didn't know why she told this girl who she barely knew, who she'd only just met and only hung out with once, about the business inside her house. Winnie didn't want anyone to know her mom was pregnant. She didn't want to think about it, either. She didn't even know when the baby was due or if her mom found out yet if it was a boy or a girl or if they had names picked out. She used to know these things, the last time her mom told her she was going to be a big sister. But they started telling Winnie less and less, and really, Winnie stopped asking.

"That's so cool," Lucía said. "I like babies. I have a lot of baby cousins."

Winnie didn't say anything.

Lucía must have channeled Pippa, though, because she kept talking. "My youngest baby cousin had his baptism last month. We all went. I don't really like watching baptisms, though? I feel bad for the baby. Gael screamed and screamed after they put water on his head."

Winnie still didn't respond.

Lucía started shifting back and forth on her feet again. "I bet you'll make a really good big sister. Better than mine anyway."

"Can you just stop?" Winnie didn't mean for it to sound so harsh, she really didn't. But she didn't want to have this conversation. It brought everything that was swirling in her gut up into her throat, a lump that sat there and made her nose burn with the threat of tears she did not want to shed in the middle of the grocery store.

"Oh." Lucía's voice was quiet, hurt. "I guess I

should go. Before my mom and sister start wondering where I am. I left them in produce."

"Wait, I'm sorry," Winnie said before Lucía turned away. "I didn't mean it. I just . . . don't like talking about it. The baby, I mean. It's a long story, and I didn't really want anyone knowing. Can you . . . maybe not tell Pippa about this?"

Lucía hesitated. Her brow creased.

"I really don't want to talk about it, Lucía. Like, ever, really. Can that just be okay?"

Lucía quickly nodded. "Yeah, sorry, of course. I'm just surprised. You were so, you know . . . *open* . . . about yourself the other night." Lucía's voice grew quieter with each word that tumbled out.

Winnie glanced around to make sure that her grandma wasn't lurking behind the glass jars or something. She probably shouldn't have been so open about *that*, either. "That's different. That's just me. That's the part that's supposed to be easy."

Lucía looked confused again. "It's not easy for me."

Winnie startled.

Lucía shrunk back. "I mean, I . . . ."

Lucía couldn't seem to find the words, but Winnie

realized she didn't need her to. She heard everything unspoken. She understood without Lucía needing to explain. "Oh," she said, still surprised, regardless, that maybe Lucía was gay, too. "You're . . ."

Lucía didn't let her ask the question. "Maybe. I mean, yes. I mean . . ."

Winnie reached out to take her hand. "It's okay."

Lucía exhaled a really deep breath. "No one knows."

"Then it's a secret for a secret," Winnie said. She held out her pinky finger. "What we said in the baby food aisle, stays in the baby food aisle."

Lucía slowly smiled at her, a small, tentative smile.

Winnie didn't hesitate smiling right back.

Lucía wrapped her pinky tightly around Winnie's.

Winnie helped her grandma bring in all the grocery bags, though she made Winnie do most of the work. Winnie attempted to help her grandma put the food away, too, but she quickly realized she didn't know where anything went, and her grandma sighed a deep, heavy sigh after Winnie asked for the fourth time in a row where something went. "I'll finish here. It'll go faster if I just put things where they go instead of having to show you every five seconds."

Which was fine by Winnie. Especially when she remembered that she hadn't FaceTimed with her mom in a few days, even though she had promised herself she would FaceTime her every morning and every night. She kept forgetting lately, which made her stomach hurt. Especially after standing in the baby food aisle, and talking with Lucía, and smiling carelessly all day.

She took the phone into her grandma's bedroom and closed the door for privacy. Her grandma didn't say anything about it, which was good, because Winnie was getting a little tired of not having any privacy.

Her mom didn't answer right away, which made Winnie's stomach hurt even more. Finally, though, she picked up. As always, her face was too close to the screen, which made it hard to tell how she was feeling. "Winnie!" her mom said. "How're you doing, bub?"

"Fine, but what about you?" Winnie asked.

"You're getting along with your grandmother?" she asked.

Winnie frowned at her. She hadn't answered Winnie's question. "I guess, but—"

"You're having fun?" her mom said, her voice

getting softer. "I just want to make sure you're having fun, and that you're getting along over there. This summer is supposed to be for you. For you to have a good time. So are you? Having a good time?"

Winnie didn't want to talk about whether or not she was having a good time. That wasn't why she called, but all the things she wanted to say she just . . . couldn't. She couldn't just ask, *Do you promise to keep smiling no matter what?* or *Do you ever think about the days when you were so sad you forgot I was even here?* or *Do you still love me, Mom, will you please just hold me?*

Really, she just wanted her mom to open her mouth and answer those questions without Winnie having to ask at all. She wanted her mom to smile at her with her beautiful smile like she used to, before the sad days, like Winnie was the most important person in her mom's world.

Instead, Winnie said, "I'm having a good time," because she knew that was what her mom needed to hear, and because—as she thought about canasta with Pippa, and the way both Pippa's and Lucía's hands felt wrapped up in hers—maybe she sort of was, sometimes anyway.

"Good, I'm glad. I know you know your grandma and I don't always get along, but it's good that you two can, you know? I'm sure you'll understand it all more when you're the one ready to move away from home." Winnie's mom paused. "Actually, no. I hope you don't. I hope I'm the kind of mom you want to live with forever."

"You'd want me around forever?"

Her mom snorted in response. "That's a silly question, Winnifred."

Was it? Then why did Winnie feel this way? If it was a silly question, what was the right one to ask to make her mom tell her dad that they needed to stop "dealing with things" without Winnie, and that they should go pick her up, and hold Winnie tight, and "deal with things" together? What was the right one to ask so that her mom would tell her she still loved her and still supported her, that Winnie didn't need to find a separate community at Pride for that? That her mom was right here, would always be here, would always smile her beautiful smile at Winnie and would never again let it all disappear?

"Things will feel normal again after the summer," her mom said, as if she could read Winnie's thoughts.

Or maybe she was having the same thoughts. "So you have fun, and things will be fine, and then soon you'll be a big sister."

Winnie was tired of being told to have fun.

And she was especially tired of being told she would be a big sister.

After the conversation with her mom, feeling all mixed up inside, Winnie left her grandma's bedroom to join her in the kitchen. She hopped up onto one of the kitchen stools, making a jingly sound come from her pocket. "Oh," she said, reaching into it and pulling out her half of the canasta winnings. "I forgot about this."

Her grandma gestured to the hollow glass turtle where she kept her own winnings. "Put it in the turtle," she said. "We'll call it our pizza fund."

Winnie blinked up at her. "Really? But you hate ordering pizza."

"Well, maybe I've changed my mind," she said. "Especially if you'll pull your weight and start helping me pay."

Winnie tried, and failed, not to smile. "Does that mean I have to keep playing canasta?"

"If you want to keep the pizza fund going, I'd say so, yes."

As Winnie rushed over to add her money to the turtle, her grandma asked, "How's your mom?"

Winnie swallowed. "Okay."

"Okay," her grandma replied.

Winnie started to count the money in the turtle, but she quickly lost count, distracted. It was mostly singles, and some change. She wondered if her grandma ever counted it. She usually just dumped her change right in. "Hey, Grandma?"

"Yes?" she said, her head deep inside the refrigerator as she moved things around to make sure everything fit.

"When is my mom supposed to have the baby?"

It got quiet, and when Winnie looked up, she realized her grandma had closed the refrigerator door and was looking back at her. "End of September."

Winnie nodded her head. "Okay."

She didn't say anything else.

Even though she really wanted to.

She wanted to say to her mom that she already had a baby, a sunshine baby. She wanted to tell her grandma that Winnie blushed around pretty girls, that Winnie had lots of crushes throughout the years on pretty girls, and she wanted her grandma not to care about any of it. She wanted her parents to tell her grandma about her mom's long, scary sad days, and she wanted them all to talk about it.

Winnie wanted to feel held. Winnie wanted to feel supported. Winnie wanted to find outside of her home what she used to feel inside but wasn't allowed to feel anymore.

Lucía had been too afraid to say the words, but Winnie hadn't been. And Winnie suddenly felt like the words might burst from her chest, hard, right here, right now, in front of her grandma, even though she wasn't supposed to do that, could not do that. Not right now. Not right here.

Winnie needed to go to Pride.

Winnie needed to be in the middle of New York City, surrounded by people who would hold her, and support her, where she could shout the words as loudly as she wanted to.

She looked back down at the money in the turtle.

Would her grandma notice if any of it was missing?

No.

No.

She couldn't do it. New York City Pride was too out of reach for her this year. The only glimpse she'd get would be the reflections of the skyscrapers off the ocean, bright white light shining off the buildings instead of rainbows.

She walked away from the hollow glass turtle and all the money inside it.

PART TWO

PRIDE (NOUN):

appreciation and respect as expressed by members of a group, typically one that has been socially marginalized, on the basis of their shared identity, culture, and experience; a public event, typically involving a parade, held to celebrate LGBTQ identities, culture, and experience.

TEN

"YOU LOOK SERIOUSLY CONTEMPLATIVE."

Winnie was, of course, sulking in her corner of the clubhouse, minding her own business. She glared up at Jeanne Strong, who never minded her own business and did so with a smile on her face. No, not a smile. A smirk. A smirk, as if Jeanne Strong knew anything. *She does*, Winnie thought, making her stomach lurch. She knows everything.

"I'm just sitting here, by myself, minding my own business," Winnie said, biting her tongue so she didn't sound like her grandma by adding: *You should do the same.*

"Where's Pippa Lai?"

"Pippa Lai had family things to do today."

Winnie briefly wondered if she should try to figure out how to bring up the fact that Jeanne *definitely* saw Winnie at Asbury Park Pride, and how she could convince Jeanne to keep her big mouth shut without sounding rude and getting into even more trouble. But before she could decide, Jeanne chucked a book onto Winnie's lap.

"What's this?" Winnie said as she picked it up.

"A book. You're going to read it."

"I'm not in book club anymore," Winnie said, even as she looked at the orange-and-black cover and flipped through the pages, liking the feel of them against her fingers. "I thought Audre Lorde was a poet. My English teacher last year was obsessed."

"Your English teacher had very good taste," Jeanne said. "She is a poet. She also wrote this. People can be more than one thing. Read that biomythography and then talk to me about it."

"What's a biomythography?"

"Read and find out."

"But I told you, I'm not in book club anymore," Winnie said again. "And, actually, I need you to—"

"Read the book anyway. We'll chat about it once you do."

Winnie scoffed. "You can't just give me homework. It's the summer. Everyone keeps saying I should have fun. And you're not, like, my teacher or grandma or anything."

Jeanne just waved her off, and Winnie was about to open her mouth and say . . . what? *Don't tell my grandma I'm gay?*

But then Pippa, who wasn't supposed to even be there, came out of nowhere to say, "What's that?" while pointing at the book still in Winnie's hands, and Jeanne left to go chat with someone else her own age.

Winnie exhaled deeply through her nose before saying, "Just some book. When did you get here? Your grandma said you weren't coming."

"I'm not staying," Pippa said, motioning out the window, where her mom's car idled in front of the clubhouse. "We wanted to drop off cookies we baked last night. And also I figured you would be here, and I wanted to tell you about the Lai Family Beach Day. We do it every year, and we're allowed to bring friends. Last year I brought . . . well, it doesn't matter. Because this year will be better."

Winnie blinked at her. As much as she was getting used to Pippa's excited way of speaking, she still didn't always have a clue what she was saying. "What's the Lai Family Beach Day?"

"Pretty much exactly what it sounds like. My family does this thing at the public beach where we all gather at my grandma's and then go over and have a barbecue and bonfire. We roast marshmallows and stuff right on the beach. Every year. We have to get a special permit for the fire and everything. It's kind of like our own holiday. But everyone is allowed to bring friends," Pippa explained, more slowly this time.

"And you're asking me to come?" Winnie asked.

Pippa shifted from one foot to the other, bouncing on her toes. "I mean, if you want to? You don't have to! It's just . . . okay, well, last year I brought friends but they spent the whole time not with me, and when I tried to hang with them they were kind of . . . well, anyway, all my cousins and aunts and everyone saw, which is why this summer my mom said I should find a new group of friends? So I thought, maybe, you and me and Lucía could go."

"Oh," Winnie said as she toyed with the pages of

the book in her lap. She shifted in the uncomfortable chair, her butt starting to hurt.

"You don't have to, though. If you don't want to. I know I'm a lot."

"Pippa, relax," Winnie said, reaching out for Pippa's arm to try to get Pippa to stop her nervous bouncing. Pippa seemed startled by the touch, and Winnie pulled her hand off, blushing. "When is it?"

"It's next week, it's always the last Sunday of June."

The same day as New York City Pride.

Not that it mattered. Winnie was perfectly free to go to Pippa's party, since she wouldn't be going anywhere else that day. "Yeah. Okay. Sounds cool."

Pippa blinked. "Really? You'll come?"

Winnie shrugged. "Yeah. You're my friend and it sounds fun."

"Great! That's so great! I'll tell everyone." Pippa's smile was huge. She glanced around the clubhouse, and then back at Winnie, and then back around the clubhouse again. "Hey, why don't you come with me and my family? We're driving to Point Pleasant to go to the boardwalk. My little brother mostly just wants to go to the aquarium, but they've got rides and stuff, too."

Winnie shook her head. "Your family is going together. I don't want to be rude."

"No! No, it's fine! Really. My little sister, Amy, will love you." She pulled Winnie up out of her chair, the book in her lap nearly falling to the floor before she caught the edge of it. "Go ask your grandma! I'll run to the car and let my mom know you're coming!"

Which was how Winnie found herself in a car full of Lais on the way to the Point Pleasant boardwalk.

The Point Pleasant boardwalk was about a half hour's drive away. Pippa's younger siblings—Amy, who was six, and Eric, who was three—spent the entire drive talking more than Pippa ever had. Which was an impressive feat, and Winnie's head was kind of spinning by the time they parked. Eric wanted to see the penguins at the aquarium—he had told Winnie this at least twelve times—so Pippa's mom said they were going to head there first. As they made their way to the entrance, Amy stuck a sticky hand into Winnie's. They had been eating snacks in the car on the way.

Jenkinson's Aquarium wasn't big, but Winnie had always liked it. She'd gone there on a school trip in fourth grade, and they'd learned the two seals they had there—Luseal and Noelani—were both rescued and couldn't be released back into the wild. They also were taught about the penguins, and who was married to who, and who was the child of who, and how many of the penguins in the aquarium were still babies, and how many of them were older than Winnie and her classmates.

The second they got inside, Amy let go of Winnie's hand so she could run and push her face against the tank filled with the big fish and sharks. Pippa leaned over the railing to peer at the turtles in their water enclosure. "I love turtles!" she said, and Winnie laughed as the turtles shrank back at the sound of her voice.

They'd made it in time to watch the penguins get fed, so they scurried over, joining the small crowd that had gathered to watch. Eric was practically buzzing, jumping up on his toes to try to see over the people in front of him. He turned around to look at Pippa, then looked over at Winnie instead. She could see him sizing her up, and she realized immediately that he'd noticed how much taller she was than Pippa. He reached for her. "Up, please!"

She glanced at Pippa for help, but Pippa was just as excited as Eric was, focused on the penguin tank.

Which left Winnie no choice. She hoisted Eric into her arms, but she quickly realized she had no idea what she was doing. He wasn't exactly sturdy; he wiggled and squirmed, and Winnie couldn't figure out how to distribute his weight so that she wasn't feeling like she was two seconds away from falling backward.

It didn't seem to deter Eric, who used his hands to push himself higher up her body, lifting his head over the crowd and clapping as they started throwing fish at the penguins. Not that *Winnie* could see.

She turned again toward Pippa, who was looking back at her this time, laughing. "I can tell you're an only child!" she said as she bent down to swiftly lift Amy up, piggyback style.

Then Winnie almost dropped Eric. He shrieked, grabbing her tightly as she readjusted her grip to hold him more securely.

She tried not to think about what Pippa said. It was true anyway. Winnie *was* an only child. She barely knew how to hold on to Eric, and she hadn't liked the feel of Amy's sticky hand in her own. Everyone could probably tell she didn't really know what she was doing, that she wanted to just put Eric down, or hand him to Pippa or his mom.

Would she someday know how to do this?

After the aquarium, they headed toward the carnival rides. Pippa had a tight grip on Eric's hand this time, and when Amy took off running, Pippa's mom called out, "Amy! Don't go too far ahead!" before turning to Pippa to add, "Go keep an eye on your sister!"

Pippa's mom took Eric into her arms and Pippa took off running after Amy, and Winnie, not knowing what else to do, took off with her.

They all made their way to the spinning teacups, after which Winnie thought she might throw up, even though the Lai kids were all shouting, "Again! Again!"

Luckily, Pippa's mom had mercy on Winnie. Though why she thought food would be a good idea after that, Winnie had no idea. Still, she bought them hot dogs and popcorn and funnel cakes. Winnie had small bites of each to be polite.

She watched Pippa's mom, and Pippa, and her siblings, as they laughed with one another. As Amy got powder on her already sticky hands and flicked it like snow onto Pippa's face. As Eric climbed into Pippa's lap. As Pippa's mom took out her phone to take a picture of the three of them, insisting that Winnie get into the picture, too.

Winnie couldn't help but wonder what it would be like to be here with her family. What would it be like to share a funnel cake with a sibling, her parents laughing and smiling with them as they made a mess together?

In the car on the way home after an exhausting afternoon, Amy fell asleep with her head on Pippa's shoulder. Winnie couldn't stop watching them. "You're good at it," she said.

"What?" Pippa asked.

"Being a big sister."

Pippa smiled. "Practice makes perfect, Winnie."

Should Winnie practice?

Should Winnie be prepared?

Maybe she could ask Pippa to teach her.

Winnie sighed, resting her head back against the seat, her forehead touching the window as she watched the trees along the Garden State Parkway go by. She couldn't ask Pippa for help. She couldn't practice, either.

Because what if she went through all the trouble, and then she didn't become a big sister again?

It was all she could think about after the Lais dropped her off at home. Her grandma blamed

Winnie's lack of appetite on junk food from the board-walk when Winnie merely picked at her dinner.

After dinner, Winnie's cell phone rang. She looked at the name, saw it was her mom, and felt panic in her chest. She hadn't spoken to her mom that day, and she should really answer the phone. But she didn't want to. She didn't want to talk to her mom. She didn't want to think about Pippa with her siblings, and how much they all smiled and laughed, and how much Winnie liked it. How much, for a moment in time, Winnie let herself think about what it could be like to be a big sister. How much, maybe, she wanted it.

Even though she didn't want it.

"Aren't you going to answer that?" her grandma asked.

Winnie shook her head.

"No?" her grandma asked, obviously surprised, eyebrows shooting up.

"No," Winnie said, as the panic in her chest pushed tighter and tighter. "No, I don't . . . *no*."

The phone stopped ringing. Or maybe she just couldn't hear it because her ears were suddenly ringing, too? Winnie scrunched up her face, realizing that her eyes were filled with tears, and she really didn't want to cry, not here, not in front of her grandma.

But her grandma was suddenly standing in front of her, holding her hands gently but tightly around Winnie's arms. "Look at me, Winnifred," she said.

Winnie shook her head.

"Hey, look at me. Just breathe. Breathe with me, Winnie."

Her grandma took a deep breath.

Winnie took one, too.

Her breath stuttered at first, and it took a couple of tries before she was able to take a really big one.

Her grandma breathed, and Winnie breathed, too, and the tightness in her chest went away, and Winnie felt herself blushing. She looked down at her feet once her tears were under control. "Sorry," she mumbled.

"Why are you apologizing?" her grandma asked.

Winnie shrugged.

"Oh, Winnie," her grandma said, and then she did something Winnie wasn't expecting. She pulled Winnie into her arms and held her tightly against her chest. Her grandma was warm and soft, and her arms felt strong. Winnie hugged her back, burying her face into her grandma's stomach.

"You've been angry since you got here," her grandma quietly said. "And I knew there were things you weren't dealing with. But this is why you're here this summer. So you can have somewhere safe just to breathe. You have a right to be angry and a right to be scared, but for now, you need to breathe, Winnie."

Winnie didn't respond.

She just let her grandma hold her, and she did her best to breathe.

ELEVEN

IT WAS FATHER'S DAY. WHICH MEANT THAT WINNIE'S MOM AND dad were taking the hour drive down to her grandma's house so that Winnie's dad could spend the day with her. When they got there, they both had smiles on their faces (thank God) and pulled Winnie in for tight hugs. Her dad even picked her up and spun her around in a circle.

Winnie tried to smile with them.

They had a reservation at a restaurant on the water where her dad had worked when he was a teenager, though it had gone through some changes since then. Winnie's grandma stayed behind, even though Winnie was tempted to ask her to please go with them. "I'll let you three have your time together," she'd said.

So it was just the three of them, sitting in a big booth next to the glass windows along the back wall with the view of the river. It was a nice day—sunny and blue—and Winnie stared out at the boats that drove by. Every so often, someone on the boat would catch her gaze and wave. Winnie never waved back.

"I've missed you, Winnie! Your grandma says you've been so busy! I hear you've been making friends and everything," her mom said. "That explains why you hardly FaceTime me anymore." She winked.

Winnie paused. Was that true?

"Winnie, get the tuna, you'll love it. Steve always made the best tuna," her dad was saying, flipping through the menu and telling both Winnie and her mom what they should or should absolutely not order, even though he wasn't even positive Steve was still working in the kitchen. He did that, though. He liked to fill the conversation with his own voice so that Winnie and her mom didn't say something to upset each other.

Winnie didn't really like fish, but her mom already took some heat for implying she was going to order the one and only chicken dish on the menu. "You don't get chicken at a fish restaurant. It's going to be dry. It's always dry," her dad said.

Winnie's mom shifted awkwardly in her seat before leaning herself on a bit of an angle. "Dry sounds perfect right now, to be honest."

He glanced down at her mom's stomach, his mood changing. "Sorry. I didn't even think."

Her mom waved him off. "No, no. It's your day, and we're fine."

"Only my day because of you and Winnie," he said.

Winnie's mom gave him one of her forced, fake smiles. It made Winnie's stomach hurt. She didn't know how she was going to eat the tuna or anything else. She turned to look back out the window.

She thought when she saw her parents again, she would be happy. She thought she'd be ready to beg them to take her home. She even made sure all her belongings were packed up into her suitcase so that when they left the next morning, she would be ready to go with them.

Now that she was here with them, though, she wasn't sure how she felt at all.

"Winnie Maude." Her dad, meanwhile, was all smiles, but they were all kind of sad. He reached for her chair and tugged it closer to him, the legs scratching against the hardwood floor, so he could wrap an arm around her. "My favorite reason for being a dad."

"I'm the only reason you're a dad," Winnie said without thinking, squirming away from his awkward side hug.

"Not for long," her mom said.

Which sent her dad into a sudden and long conversation about where the restaurant sources their fish—"Right out there, see that boat, Winnie? Right there in the bay"—so that he could make the bad moment pass as quickly as possible.

It made Winnie's stomach hurt even more.

Winnie carefully glanced up at her mom, and there was something in the expression on her mom's face that made Winnie feel scolded. She was awful at this. No wonder her mom would rather spend time shut behind the bedroom door than with her.

Winnie's dad placed a hand on her mom's stomach as the waiter came over to their table. "Now seriously, Winnie. Order the tuna."

Winnie ordered the shrimp, her mom ordered the chicken, and although they usually went for a walk along the water every time they went out for dinner, today they decided to go back to her grandma's. Her mom was tired and pale, and her dad convinced them to sit in the living room—on Winnie's bed—to watch a movie.

Her dad wrapped an arm around her mom, who in turn rested her head on his shoulder and wrapped her own arms tightly around her stomach. Winnie couldn't take her eyes off that stomach, off that round pregnant belly, as her parents watched a movie as if everything was good. As if everything was okay.

Winnie's grandma had excused herself shortly after they started the movie, which Winnie assumed was to continue giving them "family time" for Father's Day. She was sitting outside on the front porch, and Winnie didn't want to watch the movie, she didn't want to watch her parents cuddle up as if they were happy when they certainly weren't, and Winnie wasn't, either. So, quietly and without much fuss, she excused herself, too.

It was a nice day. There was a breeze coming off the water that cut through the summer heat, and the sun was low in the sky, purples and pinks and oranges cascading off the seawall and fading to night. Winnie could already see the moon.

Winnie's grandma had her eyes closed as she sat on her porch swing, head leaning back against the side of the house. "Is the movie over already?" she asked.

Winnie shook her head and sat down on the swing next to her grandma. "It's boring."

"I'm not much fun out here, either."

"It's not sad out here," Winnie said, watching the sun set behind the seawall.

Her grandma opened her eyes. "Is it sad in there?"

Winnie shrugged. She didn't know how to answer that.

"We cope how we cope, Winnie," her grandma told her, but her grandma had no idea how exactly they'd been coping, because no one had told her. She took a deep breath and then exhaled like a sigh, her shoulders settling more heavily into the back of the porch swing. "I've been thinking about your grandfather."

Winnie's grandfather had died when Winnie was little. She didn't remember him much, except for him holding her on his shoulders as he walked through the ocean up to his hips. She couldn't remember his voice, but she could still remember he'd always promise her he'd never let her go, even as the waves hit his chest, making him wobble. "What about him?" Winnie asked.

Her grandma waved her hand aimlessly in the air. "When your mom was little. How much he loved her. She was not an easy kid, let me tell you, and she could be so nasty to him when she was a teenager. I couldn't deal with her, but he was always so forgiving." Winnie's grandma laughed softly. "We were so old by then and had already raised your aunt and uncles and forgotten all about what it was like to have a teenager in the house. Your grandfather always tried, though. He'd drive your mom crazy trying to get her to hang out with him. Even if she was grumpy the whole while. You remember him, don't you?"

Winnie knew not to tell the truth. He'd been gone a long time. "Do you think about him a lot?"

Her grandma shrugged. "Sometimes more than other times, and never any real reason in between. Grief is funny like that, I guess. Hopefully, you won't need to know anything about that for a long while."

Winnie said nothing.

"Well, maybe you kind of already do," her grandma said.

Winnie didn't know why she suddenly felt like crying, or why she was flushing so hard under her grandma's gaze. "Grandma? Are you going to stay out here for a while?"

"I think so."

Winnie scooted closer to her on the swing and let herself lean back into the wood. It started moving, a bit. Gently. "Can I stay here with you?"

"You can stay with me as long as you need, Winnie." Her grandma wrapped an arm around Winnie's shoulders, and Winnie tensed for a moment, but then let herself relax. She rested her head on her grandma's shoulders, and they watched the colors in the sky fade to darkness and the stars appear.

TWELVE

"WHY DO YOU KEEP GIVING ME GAY BOOKS?" WINNIE CON-fronted Jeanne at the clubhouse the next day. Her parents had left early that morning, after kissing Winnie goodbye and telling her, again, to have fun the rest of her summer. Winnie hadn't asked to go with them.

While her parents slept the night before—her mom bunking up with her grandma in her grandma's bed, her dad on Winnie's couch, and Winnie on the floor—she couldn't get her mind to turn off. Instead, she'd reached for the book Jeanne had given her, and she started reading it.

She didn't stop reading it until the light was starting to shine through her grandma's windows come morning.

Winnie knew from her English teacher that Audre Lorde was a Black poet who wrote about identity, but she had no idea that Audre Lorde was queer. There was coincidence, and then there was Jeanne Strong, who saw Winnie at Asbury Pride and sought her out and demanded she read yet another gay book. Winnie was sure Jeanne was doing this on purpose.

She didn't even fight her grandma about tagging along that day. When her grandma got ready, so, too, did Winnie. Winnie was on a mission, and once they arrived at the clubhouse, she immediately sought out Jeanne. "I read your book last night. Audre Lorde is gay! Just like Idgie and Ruth," Winnie said, practically shoving the book back in Jeanne's hands. "I'm not stupid, you're doing this on purpose."

"Did you like the book?" Jeanne asked.

Winnie loved it, but that wasn't the point. "You saw me at Asbury, at Pride."

"I almost didn't recognize you!" Jeanne said, smiling. "And not just because of the rainbow face paint.

Your face! You were all sunshine and happiness there for a while. I don't think I'd ever seen you smile before."

"You can't tell my grandma we were there. You didn't tell my grandma, did you?" Winnie paused, suddenly realizing something. "*You* were at Pride. Does my grandma know that you . . . ?"

"I've been queer for about a thousand years, Winnie. Your grandma most certainly knows. She knew my wife, too, matter of fact," Jeanne said.

Winnie felt a little bit like she needed to sit down. "My grandma knows . . . ?" Jeanne nodded. Winnie's grandma knew. Was that the real reason her grandma didn't like Jeanne? Because she was gay? Because she had a wife? Was Winnie's mom right to worry that Winnie's grandma would hurt her, too?

Would her grandma hurt her?

Winnie thought they were starting to get along, but . . .

But . . .

"You can't tell my grandma you saw me there. And you need to stop giving me these books! She'll figure it out eventually if I keep having gay books around the house!"

"I thought you were just being all preteen about

your reaction to *Fried Green Tomatoes*, but then I saw you and I *got it*," Jeanne said. "I see you, Winnie. So, if you're not ready now, you come to me when you are. You can talk to me. Okay?"

Winnie was sweating. This was too much. "You have to say that you won't tell my grandma."

"It's hard when your family doesn't know."

"My family knows, and it's none of your business," Winnie said, but suddenly felt the urge to explain anyway. "I'm not in the closet. I'm *not*. I've been gay for a thousand years, too, okay, and I know what I'm doing and who I am and you can stop butting in now."

"You're angry," Jeanne said. "And I get that. I would never tell your grandma, or anyone for that matter, if that's what you need. But, Winnie, it's okay. You know that, right?"

All Winnie knew was that she didn't want to stay here, with Jeanne, with her grandma, and she didn't want to go home, with her mom, and there was nowhere else for her to go. "Are you going to Pride in the city?" she asked.

Jeanne shook her head. "Oh, no. I don't do the big one anymore."

"One day I will. I'll go and it'll be fine because *I'm*

fine," Winnie said before she could stop herself. "I'm not hiding, and I'm not angry, and I don't need your help or your books."

She left Jeanne and the book behind and stomped out the front door of the clubhouse.

THIRTEEN

"WE'VE BEEN SCROLLING THROUGH NETFLIX FOR, LIKE, EVER. Just pick one," Winnie said to Pippa, as she, Lucía, and Pippa all sat around Pippa's living room looking for something to watch.

Pippa couldn't make up her mind, and Lucía hated making decisions, and Winnie didn't really give a hoot, so they were endlessly scrolling.

But then Winnie spoke as Pippa scrolled past *Fried Green Tomatoes*. "Wait, wait. Stop. That one."

"*That* one?" Pippa asked, eyebrows raised.

"I read the book," Winnie said. Neither Pippa nor

Lucía looked all that convinced. "It's not like you had any better options, just trust me."

Winnie had received a formal phone call invitation from Pippa's grandma to Winnie's grandma for Winnie to come over for what they kept referring to as a "playdate." She had to assume Lucía's family got a similar call. When they got there, they were told to take off their shoes and sit in the living room, and Pippa's grandma and mom had both come in numerous times since they'd gotten there to ask if they wanted anything, if everything was okay, and to say how happy they were that Lucía and Winnie were there.

Winnie didn't think they were used to having people over all that often.

They even made sure that Pippa's siblings left them alone, even though Winnie kind of found herself wishing they hadn't done that.

Winnie was glad to get out of her house. She didn't want to be with her grandma right now. She was still on edge over her conversation with Jeanne, who kept waving at her from across the street no matter how quickly Winnie turned to look away.

She just wanted to sit around with her friends and

not have to worry so much about anything. So when Mrs. Lai had called, Winnie said *yes* faster than even her grandma could.

The distraction was only kind of working. Winnie kept her cell phone in her sweaty hand, going back and forth on whether or not she wanted to text Maria: *My grandma's neighbor saw us at pride and my grandma hates her and what if she'd hate me, too.*

"Was the book good?" Lucía asked as Pippa clicked on the movie.

It took Winnie a second to realize what Lucía was talking about. She could only nod in response; the lump in her throat made it hard to swallow.

Winnie needed the distraction. So when Pippa hit play and the movie started, Winnie tried to lean back into the Lais' couch and just . . . watch the movie, with her friends, like normal. Like nothing was happening inside her home or outside her home, and life was just this moment, right here.

But Winnie quickly realized something wasn't right (other than Pippa complaining that it was too old and they should have picked something better). The movie—though it *was* good—was *not* like the book. Well, it *was* like the book but it . . . *wasn't.* Winnie watched as Idgie and Ruth were Idgie and Ruth, but weren't Idgie and Ruth at all.

It broke Winnie's heart when Pippa said, "I've always wanted a best friend like that."

Because in the movie, Idgie and Ruth *were* just best friends. Idgie and Ruth, who were *in love* in the book, were *just friends* in the movie. The movie changed that—erased it. Winnie watched, hoping it would somehow be different, and suddenly they'd be in love for real, but it never did.

They hid their real relationship in the movie—maybe they kept it behind closed doors, kept their relationship *inside* their home instead of outside, on the screen for everyone to see—and Winnie was *tired*. Winnie was *so tired* of feeling this way.

Winnie was already crying before the point in the movie when Ruth died, but that was when Pippa and Lucía noticed. And Winnie didn't stop crying after the movie ended—she couldn't—and Winnie had never cried in front of Lucía and Pippa before (she rarely cried *ever* anymore), but she couldn't stop, because Idgie and Ruth were only best friends in the movie and her grandma hated Jeanne Strong who once had a wife and went to Pride, and Winnie was not supposed to talk about anything and she'd just wanted a distraction from all of it.

Instead, it felt like someone had kicked her hard, right in the stomach.

"Are you okay?" Pippa asked as the credits rolled.

"I'm just tired, or whatever," Winnie said, wiping her face. "I should go home. I'll talk to you later, okay?"

"Wait, Winnie, what's wrong, don't go," Pippa said, reaching for Winnie's arm. "Tell us, maybe we can help."

"I just need to go. I'll call you tomorrow. Okay?"

Winnie ignored Pippa's protests and found Pippa's mom in the kitchen to tell her she was leaving.

"Do you want me to call your grandmother?"

Absolutely not. "It's okay. She knows I'm walking home," Winnie said, which was only sort of true, but she was getting used to all the half lies lately. She hurried out the door before Pippa's mom could change her mind and make Winnie call her grandma to come get her.

She just wanted to be alone.

She was already all the way up Pippa's street by the time she heard Lucía call after her. "Winnie! Wait up!" Winnie didn't stop walking—the cool ocean breeze was sharp against her face as she moved, which Winnie liked because it took the tears right out of her eyes and stung her cheeks until it made them numb— but she did slow down. Lucía was out of breath when she caught up to her.

"Why are you following me?" Winnie asked.

"I thought I'd walk home with you," Lucía said. "If that's okay."

Winnie wanted to say no. She shrugged instead. As much as she wanted to be alone . . . she didn't *really* want to be alone.

Lucía lived farther down the road, outside of the senior citizen community, but Winnie's grandma's house was pretty close to Pippa's grandma's place, separated by Jeanne Strong's house and three others. Instead of walking straight to her grandma's, though, Winnie turned to head toward the main road, toward the direction of the ocean, going out of her way to walk along the seawall.

Lucía followed her.

The breeze was cooler, harsher, on the wall, thick still with humidity and salt. Winnie looked out at the ocean. It was too dark to see the horizon line, to tell where the sand met water, or where the ocean ended and the sky began. She could hear the waves crashing, though, and the moon reflected off the water, so Winnie knew the shore was still there, as well as the beach, the sand, the rocks, and the sea glass.

"They were supposed to be gay," Winnie said, breaking the silence that had followed them from Pippa's house.

"Who?" Lucía asked.

"Idgie and Ruth," Winnie said. "The movie ruined it."

"Oh," Lucía said.

"Why does everyone do this?" Winnie asked. "No one talks about things that matter. They make everyone bottle them up and pretend they don't exist, or say it's no one else's business. But it's my business! *Mine!* And my parents never once ask if I need to talk about it. They don't care if I need to talk about any of it."

"What do you need to talk about, Winnie?" Lucía asked.

Winnie turned away from the dark horizon and into Lucía's big brown eyes instead. Lucía was listening. She was looking at Winnie, not out at the ocean or the sky or anything but Winnie. And, yes, Lucía was outside of Winnie's home. Winnie was not supposed to tell her anything. But . . . she wanted to. She realized suddenly it felt *right* to. "Did you know that I'm a sunshine baby? I didn't know what that was, but I think it means that I might only ever be sort of a big sister and never actually a big sister. And I tried not to want to be a big sister, but I think I kind of do, and I can't want that. Because I don't know what's going to happen this time. What if it's so much worse this time?"

Winnie was looking down at her feet. She couldn't look at Lucía's eyes, not when saying all this both made Winnie feel much better and also made her feel like she was betraying something, too. "My mom gets so sad. And I get it! It's *so* sad! I was so sad when she didn't have the other babies, too, but my mom forgot how to smile and she forgot how to be my mom because she couldn't be someone else's mom, too, and I don't want to lose her again. I just got her back, and right when I got her back they said she was having a baby, again, and then they told me to stay with my grandma, and what if my mom only stopped being sad because she could have another baby? Why couldn't she just stop being sad for me?"

"Your mom loves you, Winnie," Lucía said. "My mom always wanted a big family. She kept wanting more and more of us, but that doesn't mean my older sisters weren't good enough. It just means that I get to be here, too."

"My mom and my grandma fight a lot. My mom was worried my grandma would hurt me if she knew I was gay. I think my grandma likes me a lot, now, and I thought we were getting closer, even though I didn't want anything to do with her when I first got here, but she hates her neighbor Jeanne, and Jeanne is gay, so now I'm nervous." Winnie brought a hand up to roughly wipe at her face. The wind wasn't doing a good job anymore of keeping her tears from falling. "I've never been nervous before. But now I'm nervous about my mom and my grandma and I just wanted to feel held. That's all I wanted."

"Winnie . . ." Lucía placed a hand on Winnie's shoulder. Winnie didn't flinch away, but she stood ramrod straight, her hands in fists at her sides, trying to stop her tears from falling. She shook her head, once, twice, trying to tell Lucía that she couldn't say anymore. She'd already said too much, had thrown open her household doors for Lucía's ears, and her throat was tight, and she was done now.

Lucía stood there, her hand warm on Winnie's shoulder, as they listened to the waves crashing against the sand. No one was allowed on the beaches at night. Police officers sometimes patrolled to make sure of it, to chase teens off it, to keep everyone safe from how darkly the sky buried the water, hid it from sight.

"There are things I wish I could say, too. But I know that I can't, no matter how much I want to," Lucía suddenly said, and Winnie turned to look at her, to show that she would listen, too. Lucía took a deep breath before she continued. "I want everyone to like me as much as they like my sisters, and I think that they'll like me even less if they ever find out that I like girls."

"I don't like you less," Winnie said. "I actually might like you more."

Lucía smiled.

Winnie smiled, too.

The two of them stood that way, next to each other, watching the dark beach, listening to the crashing waves, until the wind died down and the little gnats came out and they both knew they had no choice but to go home.

Winnie got home with skinned, bloody knees, the result of a bit of a spill down the seawall. Her shoe had gotten caught on a protruding sharp rock, and she basically slid down halfway on her knees before she managed to catch herself.

She refused to cry *again* in front of Lucía, especially since she had finally just stopped, but by the time they separated, heading in the directions of their own homes, Winnie was wincing with each awkwardly stiff step. There was sand caked into the sticky blood on her skin, which she only made worse when she tried to rub it away. She would not cry over skinned knees, seawall be damned.

Except, she already kind of was.

Winnie's grandma was sitting on the couch, wrapped in the blankets Winnie slept with, when Winnie walked into her house. The lights were out, except for the TV, which cast a glowy-blue light on the living room, and Winnie hoped it would cover her tear-stained face and bloody knees.

The lack of light did nothing to cover the little whimper that escaped Winnie's throat as she stepped over the threshold, which caught her grandma's attention immediately. "What's wrong?" she asked. The blanket was hooked around her shoulders as she got up off the couch and quickly made her way over to Winnie. "Your knees! What happened?"

"Nothing," Winnie mumbled. "I fell, but I'm fine."

"Come here, come sit down," her grandma said, and Winnie let her pull her to the couch.

Her grandma lifted up one of Winnie's legs.

"Ow! Wait, don't!"

"I need to clean this, Winnie. You'll get an infection. It's filled with sand."

Her grandma went into the bathroom for her first aid kit, and Winnie watched in wonder as she did. She couldn't remember the last time she even so much as asked her parents for a Band-Aid. Winnie knew better than to make a fuss over scrapes and scratches, all things considered.

Her grandma knelt in front of Winnie, and it looked awfully uncomfortable for her to be on her knobby knees that she complained about so often when they walked the short distance to the clubhouse. "You don't have to, I can do it," Winnie said, reaching for her grandma's arm to maybe steady her and help her stand back up. But her grandma ignored her, dabbing at Winnie's knees. The alcohol swab burned, and Winnie squirmed, again fighting a losing battle with tears.

"Hey, it's okay," her grandma said, leaning over to blow lightly on Winnie's scrapes. Winnie froze as her grandma's warm breath tickled her skin, giving her goose bumps. She watched her move close, her lips right above Winnie's knees, her eyes closed as she blew gently where it stung. It didn't really do much to make anything feel better but . . . also it kind of did. Winnie's grandma's hand, as it rubbed along the back of Winnie's calf, felt nice, too.

Winnie held her breath, not wanting anything to interrupt this moment. She didn't want to give her grandma any reason to stop.

But Winnie looked at her grandma's face, noticing how she cringed as she shifted on her knees. "You should, I mean, should you come sit down?" Winnie asked.

"Let me finish taking care of you quick and then

I'm absolutely going to shove you over for a spot on that couch," her grandma replied as she gently smoothed out the Band-Aid over Winnie's knee.

Her grandma did have trouble getting back up, and Winnie held out her hands for her grandma to use as ballast. She practically flopped right down next to Winnie, her weight unbalancing the couch cushion enough that Winnie had no choice but to lean into her side. Her grandma, with both hands, wiped away the sandy tears on Winnie's cheeks.

"Oh, my Winnifred," her grandma said. "What on earth can I say to keep you off the seawall?"

It struck Winnie, suddenly, how Lucía now knew Winnie better than her grandma did. And so did Maria, and so did Pippa, and so, even, did Jeanne Strong. Her grandma barely knew her at all. She only knew the part of Winnie that her parents allowed her to show outside of their walls. There was a big part of her that her grandma might never learn about, a part of Winnie that Winnie didn't even really know how to exist without.

Her grandma could never truly know her. So she could never really hold her, either.

Her grandma started wiping Winnie's cheeks again. "You're crying—do your knees still really hurt?"

Winnie shook her head. Her knees were fine. "No. I'm just, I don't know. Tired, I guess."

Winnie's grandma pulled away and patted Winnie's thigh. "I'll leave you to your couch and head on into bed, then."

Which wasn't what Winnie meant at all. She wanted to ask her grandma to stay and hold her and make all the pain go away, but she said nothing as her grandma carefully stood from the couch. Winnie awkwardly held out a hand to help when she saw her grandma wince, but she didn't take it this time. "Don't stay up watching TV all night. Get some sleep."

Winnie turned off the TV once her grandma closed her bedroom door. She was surprised how quickly after she fell asleep.

FOURTEEN

PRIDE WAS ONLY A WEEK AWAY. WINNIE COUNTED DOWN THE days as if she were going to go. She couldn't help it. It stuck in her head, and morning after morning she'd wake up and think, *One day closer.*

It didn't help that Pippa's party was the same day, and the first thing out of Pippa's mouth that day was, "The Lai Family Beach Day is only a week away!"

Winnie sat on one of the plastic beach chairs that lined the pool at the pool club, shifting her weight every so often to avoid sticking to the plastic as the sun shone hotly. Pippa, as usual, was the only one of them who actually wanted to go *in* the pool. Winnie scrolled through the calendar on her phone, putting in Pippa's party and deleting Pride before scrolling to the following year. It felt so far away, and Winnie couldn't help but wonder what would be different by then. Her mom wouldn't be pregnant anymore, that was certain; Winnie's grandma said she was due at the end of September, which was only a few months away.

Winnie didn't want to think about that, though.

"Winnie!" Pippa splashed from the water, but she was too far to reach Winnie and ended up soaking Lucía instead, who was sitting at the very edge of the beach chair. "Your phone's gonna overheat in the sun—come into the pool!"

Winnie picked at the corner of the now-wet Band-Aid her grandma had carefully placed over the scab on her knee just this morning.

"I don't swim in pools," Winnie said for the umpteenth time.

"Will you swim in the ocean on Sunday?" Pippa asked. "For my family's beach barbecue? Please say you will. Wear a bathing suit at least, just in case you decide to."

"I don't swim, *period*," Winnie clarified. "Especially in the ocean."

"At least put your feet in," Pippa said.

Lucía bumped her shoulder against Winnie's, giving her a small smile. "It's okay. We can stay on the sand together."

Winnie blushed, tucking her head down, trying to hide her smile.

Ever since they watched *Fried Green Tomatoes* together and walked along the seawall and confessed the things they wished they could talk about and talked about those things with each other, Winnie noticed Lucía's smile a lot more. Or maybe Lucía was just smiling more.

Winnie wanted to share her smiles with Lucía.

Lucía would like Pride. Maybe if Maria took Winnie next year, Lucía could go with them. They could both feel held together.

Pippa splashed them again. Lucía shrieked and ducked away from the water, laughing, as Winnie rolled her eyes. "You guys are too far," Pippa whined. "At least come sit on the edge of the pool!"

Winnie and Lucía put their legs into the pool, and Winnie had to admit that the water felt good. It seemed to satisfy Pippa for a moment, as she did somersaults under the water.

At least if Winnie couldn't go to Pride, she had Pippa's party. She was looking forward to Pippa's mom doting on them, to Pippa trying again to get her and Lucía to swim in the ocean. She was even looking forward to Eric and Amy with their sticky hands and their loud voices. And she was definitely looking forward to getting to spend more time making Lucía smile and making Pippa happy and maybe actually having fun and being happy, too.

"Pippa's right over there again!"

"Oh no! Abort, abort!"

Winnie turned her head at the sound of the voices she was getting all too familiar with, for girls she didn't even know. They were cackling, covering their mouths like they were trying to be polite, even though they weren't at all as they made fun of Pippa while Pippa was *right here.*

Pippa had popped her head out of the water and was holding on to the edge of the pool, smile gone, watching the girls laugh at her.

It wasn't fair for these girls, who Pippa wasn't even bothering, to steal Pippa's smiles so often.

It *wasn't fair* that these girls didn't know how hard it was sometimes to get smiles back once you took them away.

"*Relax*," Winnie snapped in their direction. "She doesn't even want to hang out with you anyway!"

Lucía went stiff beside Winnie, and Pippa seemed to freeze, also, wide eyes looking up at Winnie from the pool. The girls were staring at Winnie, too, before one of them—the one, as usual, in front of the rest of them—crossed her arms around her chest. "Who even *are* you?" she said.

"I'm Winnie Nash," she said, narrowing her eyes. "Can you leave us alone? We're having plenty of fun without you."

One of the other girls started giggling, which earned her a glare from the others. But with a roll of her eyes, the girl in the front did turn around and start heading in the direction of the beach, away from the pool. The rest of them followed her. They broke out into giggles and whispers, and Winnie knew they were probably still talking about them, were probably still going to make fun of Pippa, but at least they weren't doing it *here*, right now, anymore.

When Winnie turned to look at Pippa, to try to

figure out how she was feeling, Pippa was scrambling to push herself up and out of the water. She dripped all over Winnie, who was about to tell her to stop standing so close, but then Pippa's arms wrapped tightly around her in a hug. She held on to Winnie, getting pool water all over her. Winnie had to put a hand behind her on the concrete to keep them both from rolling over.

"Thank you, Winnie," Pippa said right into Winnie's ear. "You're the best friend ever."

Winnie flushed, glancing over at Lucía. She was smiling at Winnie, too.

Pippa pulled back and said, "Now will you *please* come into the pool?"

Winnie laughed. "No! No pools!"

"You two are so boring!" Pippa shouted, as she jumped back in and started splashing at them again.

"I'm not boring! I'm the best friend ever!" Winnie shouted, and started kicking her feet as fast as she could, and Lucía joined in, kicking faster, faster, faster, with a big smile on her face, and Pippa had to dive back under the water, laughing so hard she probably would start choking, to avoid the splashing they fired back at her. Winnie loved the sound of their laughter.

She loved the way her own laughter sounded with them, too.

She needed Pride, that was true. She needed the Pride community to hold her.

But she had something for her here, too.

On Saturday morning (*One more sleep until the party!!!!* Pippa had texted first thing), Winnie's grandma was banging around so loudly in the kitchen that Winnie didn't stand a chance of being able to stay asleep on the couch. She picked her head up and watched as her grandma opened the refrigerator, stared into it, and then closed it. She proceeded to do the same thing with all the cabinets before moving to the counter, where she had a newspaper and a pad and started scribbling notes.

"Oh, good, you're awake," her grandma said when she caught sight of Winnie's head poking up over the arm of the couch, as if she weren't making enough noise to wake the neighbors, let alone the twelve-year-old who didn't have a bedroom to hide in. "You are eating me out of house and home. Go get dressed—we need to get to the grocery store before the morning crowd hits. That parking lot is impossible come noon on the weekends."

"Ugh, no thanks," Winnie said, her voice muffled as she pressed her head back into her pillow, covering herself with her blanket. "I'm sleeping."

Her grandma didn't respond, so Winnie thought—foolishly—she was in the clear as she settled back in comfortably. No sooner did she feel herself relax than her blanket suddenly went flying off her. Shocked, Winnie sat up to see her grandma, a big, joyful smirk on her face, hand raised and holding the blanket she'd ripped off Winnie like a magician.

"Grandma!"

"Oh, good, you're awake," her grandma pointedly repeated.

Winnie unsuccessfully tried to fight back a smile. "I'm not. You're dreaming."

Her grandma leaned in close, and Winnie braced herself, wondering for a moment if her grandma would pull her right off the couch as easily as she did the blanket.

She went for Winnie's stomach instead, fingers wiggling relentlessly as she tickled Winnie—hard. Winnie immediately shrieked, laughing and squirming with no room to escape on the couch. "Grandma! No, no, no!" Her grandma stopped right around the first no, moving to pat Winnie on the leg instead as Winnie's laughter died down.

Her grandma kept smiling. "Now, that's a sound we don't get much around here."

"I don't laugh," Winnie said, though she could feel the smile still on her face. "I save all my laughter up."

"Save it for what? Let it out, Winnifred. It's a beautiful sound that you deserve to feel and I deserve to hear," her grandma said. "Now get up. I'm serious about beating the crowds."

When they got back home from the grocery store, Winnie—not wanting to have to take more trips to and from the car than necessary—made it a mission to carry as many of the grocery bags as possible in one go. She looped all the bag handles up her arms, starting with the paper products and produce and meats, leaving the extra-heavy bags with all the canned goods in them for her grandma to take.

Her grandma's cell phone started ringing, so she stayed by the car as she answered it, fiddling with the receipt she put in her pocketbook while Winnie made her way up to the front door.

"*What's wrong?*"

Her grandma's voice was so sharp into the phone, Winnie froze. She turned, bags of groceries still in her hands starting to weigh her down.

"Kit, slow down."

It was Winnie's mom.

"It's okay. You're okay," her grandma said into the phone, but Winnie didn't think she sounded much like she believed it. "Call nine-one-one. I'll call Nick. We'll meet you at the hospital."

Winnie's arms started to burn, and she felt the bags slip. She couldn't move, and the food spilled out at her feet.

"What's wrong?" Winnie's voice sounded small and muffled in her ears.

"We need to hurry and put this stuff away. Your mom . . . we're going to meet her at the hospital. Careful, Winnie, the food is all over the porch."

Winnie still couldn't move.

This all sounded too familiar.

Winnie used to dream about being a big sister. She wanted someone to play with, to go to the beach with.

She would help teach them that the little holes in the shells on the beach that made them perfect for necklaces were made by tiny snails, and teach them how to fold a slice of pizza so that the grease didn't pour down their arms as they walked along the boardwalk. She wouldn't feel so lonely when her mom and dad both had to work.

She would read them *Harriet the Spy* and *Raymie Nightingale* and all her favorite books. She would confide that she had a crush on Kissin' Kate Barlow in *Holes*. She would learn how to hold the baby carefully so that their neck was supported, and she would continue to hold them as they grew up, just like Pippa knew how. She would be the best big sister. She would.

But she hadn't had those dreams in a while. She wouldn't let herself have them. Because she had been here before, right here, had done this before with her mom. She felt like she had been holding her breath, waiting for this moment, and now it was here.

She wasn't ready.

Winnie was having trouble breathing. She focused instead on the groceries that were scattered all over between Winnie's feet and the porch, blueberries spilled out of their containers, the packaged meat wet and leaking on the ground, a loaf of bread smooshed under the weight of the bag that fell on top of it.

"Winnie, come help me."

Her grandma locked eyes with Winnie, and she immediately stopped barking orders, quickly making her way to Winnie. "Okay," she said, grabbing Winnie's chin. "Okay. Look at me. Drop the rest of those bags, okay? I'm going to bring them inside, and then we'll head to the hospital. You're okay, Winnie. It's going to be okay. All right?"

Winnie must have nodded, because her grandma nodded back and suddenly seemed so strong and so capable as she moved around Winnie, picking up all the spilled food, and Winnie didn't remember much else except for her grandma's arms wrapping tight around Winnie as she picked her up and carried her to the car.

Winnie's grandma was talking to the doctor when her dad arrived. Winnie was sitting in a row of light blue waiting room chairs along the back wall, next to a water cooler and a stack of old magazines. "Winnie!"

He immediately rushed over to her. "What happened, where's your grandma?"

Winnie said nothing, because what even could she say? She had no idea what had happened. No one told her anything, no one ever told her anything. Not what happened or what *was* happening. She hadn't seen her mom yet, and she wasn't even sure if she *wanted* to see her. Her grandma pulled her dad away from her and out of sight to explain things out of Winnie's earshot anyway. Winnie watched as her dad then found a doctor to explain things to him, too.

Maria was now there, too, though Winnie wasn't sure when she'd shown up or how long she'd even been there. The waiting room was busy but not full. The TV on the wall was playing afternoon soap operas, and Winnie had spent most of the time staring at the ugly carpet ever since her grandma had pulled her into the hospital.

Winnie wanted her mom. She wanted to sit in her mom's lap and feel her mom's arms and see her mom's smile, her beautiful smile, and she wanted someone to tell her that everything would be okay. That this nightmare that Winnie and her family kept having over and over and over again would end okay.

Maria didn't seem to hesitate the moment she saw Winnie sitting alone, and she rushed to her side to sit in the chair next to her. She pulled Winnie into her arms as she glanced around, probably looking for any sight of Winnie's dad or grandma. "What happened, Winnie?" she asked, but Winnie still didn't have any answers to give her.

Maria held Winnie close and tight, kissing her hair as she softly started singing, "You are my sunshine, my only sunshine, you make me happy when skies are gray . . ."

Winnie closed her eyes and listened to Maria's voice, trying to ignore the way the light above them was flickering just enough to give Winnie a headache, and how the man four chairs over kept coughing something phlegmy and gross-sounding.

Winnie had smiled so much lately. She had laughed so much just this morning.

She was careless. She was *stupid*.

"You'll never know, dear, how much I love you . . ."

Winnie wanted to tell Maria to stop singing that song. Because she wasn't anyone's sunshine, she *wasn't*, and Winnie didn't want to do this anymore. She couldn't remember what her mom's laughter sounded like, and she wanted to ask Maria if she did, if she could tell Winnie right now how it sounded so Winnie could have that in her ears instead.

But she was afraid if she opened her mouth to say anything at all, she would just start screaming.

FIFTEEN

AT SOME POINT, WINNIE FELL ASLEEP. SHE WOKE UP ALONE, curled up along three of those light blue waiting room chairs. She immediately sat up, eyes darting around the room trying to find someone she knew.

She saw no one except for strangers sitting scattered throughout the rest of the light blue chairs, filling out paperwork and playing on their phones and staring and waiting. The TV hung up in the corner was playing *General Hospital* without the sound on, and no one was watching it. Someone cleared their throat, and someone else was crying quietly, and someone else was holding a towel-covered hand, stained red, up above their head. The few phone conversations Winnie could overhear were various versions of "She's still back there" or "The doctor won't talk to me" or "I've been waiting for over two hours" or "Please come quickly."

Winnie gripped the edge of the seat tightly, clenching her teeth together and breathing deeply through her nose. She did not want to be left alone.

Her heart thumped wildly at the thought of being left behind, and her stomach hurt, and her throat locked up tight, until she finally spotted her grandma at reception, talking to the woman behind the desk. Winnie wanted to run to her, but she couldn't get herself to move very quickly at all. She felt weighted down as she slowly stood and crossed the stained carpet of the waiting room to get to the other side. Her grandma, clipboard and pen in hand, immediately stopped writing to wrap an arm around Winnie's shoulders, and Winnie could breathe a little easier again.

"Your mom works in a damn hospital, and *still* her insurance is a mess," Winnie's grandma said.

"What's wrong with my mom?"

The sound Winnie's grandma made as she exhaled

made it seem as if she had nothing left to breathe. "They're trying to pinpoint exactly what the problem is. Right now they think—"

"Did you get it sorted?" Winnie's dad was suddenly right behind her, interrupting and leaning over to see the clipboard in Winnie's grandma's hand. He glanced down at Winnie. "Oh, good, you're up."

Oh, good, you're awake. Was it really just that morning her grandma had woken her up, banging around, yanking the blanket off her, tickling her and making her smile and making her laugh and making her think the day would be normal?

"Your mom wants to see you, come on, Winnie Maude," her dad said, his hand firm on her arm as he started to lead her toward the swinging doors. The ones currently closed tightly, separating the waiting room from everything inside.

Winnie didn't want this.

She didn't want to see her mom's face, sad like before.

She didn't want to do this again. She did not want to go back there, through the closed doors to the other side, and do this again.

"No."

Her dad nearly stumbled, turning to look at her with disbelief all over his face. "What do you mean, no? Your mom's awake and asking for you."

Winnie felt like she was drowning in the ocean, sinking lower, lower, lower. *"No."*

"It's okay, Winnie," her grandma said, placing her hand on Winnie's shoulder, making Winnie jump.

None of this was okay. Not a single thing was okay, and of course they wouldn't talk about that, because they never talked about anything. "No. I don't want to. *No.*"

"She needs you right now, Winnifred, don't be like this. We talked about this."

Someone cleared their throat, followed up with an *excuse me*, and Winnie's dad tugged her away from the reception desk window that they were currently blocking.

"Knock it off. Stop being selfish," Winnie's dad said.

And the feeling that had been pushing down on her chest, that had been making her clench her jaw and push her fingernails into her palms, came bursting out.

Winnie found her voice and started shouting, "I'm not selfish! Mom is selfish! *You're* selfish!"

"Hey! Lower your voice!" her dad said as he raised his. "Did you completely forget where we are right now?"

"I didn't forget, and we're only here because of you! Because of you and Mom and not me! I've been good! I haven't told anyone anything like you told me not to and I've saved all my smiles for Mom so she could have them and no one asked me what I wanted, but *I don't want to see her*!"

Two strong arms suddenly came around her, and she was pulled into the solid weight of her grandma as her grandma held her tight, so tight that even though Winnie started fighting against it, she stopped, surrendering to its warmth. Her grandma had her hand pressed gently on Winnie's dad's chest, a firm but soothing gesture that kept him steadied at a distance.

"This is a lot, and not helping anyone," Winnie's grandma said to her dad. "Go be with Kit. I'm going to call Grace Lai to see if Winnie can stay with them for the night. She's been in the hospital all day. Let her spend time with her friend and then I'll bring her back tomorrow. You're both all worked up right now. You and I will sort out this insurance stuff, and Winnie can see Kit when she's ready."

Winnie was surprised by how young her dad seemed as her grandma told him what to do. It also surprised her how easily he agreed.

"Okay. I'm sorry. It's okay, Winnie. I love you." He gave her a hug and held on almost too tight.

Winnie didn't hold him back at all.

Winnie thought she would feel better once she left the hospital. She thought she would be able to breathe easier without the threat of having to see her mom's face, thought she could see Pippa and listen to Pippa talk about whatever, and she would stop shivering, would stop feeling like she might explode. But she just kept feeling something tight in her chest, and her arms and legs, and she clenched and unclenched her fists as she lay in the makeshift bed Pippa's grandma made for her on the floor of Pippa's room, staring up at the ceiling.

They'd stopped at Winnie's grandma's house first.

The mess from the groceries that her grandma hadn't had time to clean after putting the rest of the groceries away was still there. Her grandma scooped up the blueberries that were all over the porch. Winnie stood dazedly by the kitchen table, staring at the hollow glass turtle that held all the money Winnie and her grandma had won from canasta. Winnie reached over to touch it, her fingers grazing along the paper bills, scratchy against her skin.

How much money did it take to get to the city?

It happened without thought, it really did, because the next thing Winnie knew, they were on their way to Pippa's grandma's house and Winnie had all the money from the turtle in her pocket, some of it earned while smiling and laughing with Pippa and a bunch of senior citizens.

Smiles and laughter she should never have given away.

Pizza money wasn't worth it.

But maybe finally getting to the city was.

Pippa was talking faster than usual, as if she wanted to fill up Winnie's bad feelings with chatter, instead. "I know you're upset. I wish I could make it better," Pippa said, which she had told Winnie nearly ten times already since she walked through the door. "Hey, Winnie?" she continued, because apparently Pippa didn't believe in sleeping during sleepovers.

"What?"

"Why didn't you tell me your mom was pregnant?"

Winnie wished her grandma had called Lucía's parents instead. Lucía already knew about Winnie's mom's pregnancy, but also already knew that Winnie did not want to talk about it. She certainly wouldn't be asking about it, not while Winnie lay on the floor biting the inside of her cheek to keep everything locked inside of her.

Winnie turned over to face the opposite direction from Pippa's bed, and that's when she saw it, up on Pippa's dresser, placed right in the center of the wood: the smooth blue piece of sea glass she and Pippa found the first time they walked along the seawall together.

Winnie didn't want to look at that sea glass. She didn't want to think about all the times she smiled with Pippa and Lucía since then.

"I'm your friend, Winnie," Pippa said. "I don't understand why you didn't tell me. Your mom is having a baby! That's so exciting. I can teach you all about being a big sister!"

Winnie shut her eyes tightly. Maybe everything would be better come morning. "Just go to bed, Pippa. I'm tired." She stuck her hand into her pajamas pocket, gripping the dollar bills tight in her hand, wrinkling them as the edges scratched against her skin.

"I know you have a lot on your mind right now," Pippa said, her voice a near whisper. "But I would still very much like if you could come to my party tomorrow. Lucía and me, we'll take care of you. We can distract you from worrying too much about your mom. We'll make sure you're okay."

Winnie had been looking forward to that party. She'd been looking forward to laughing, and smiling, and being held by her friends.

She was so stupid. She had been so careless with her smiles all summer.

"Leave me alone, Pippa. *Please.*" Winnie hated the cracked sound in her voice, hated how weak and tired she felt lying in Pippa's bedroom.

But for the first time since Winnie had known her, Pippa fell quiet.

Winnie gripped the money tight in her sweaty hand, closed her eyes, and waited for morning.

Winnie woke up to a text from her grandma at 8:02 a.m.

> Your mom is doing okay. They ran some tests and we're going to find out what's wrong soon. Do you want me to come get you?

Winnie didn't want to be there when they found out what was wrong. She didn't want to see her mom's face when she heard, didn't want to see her grandma's or dad's faces, either. She was too afraid of how quickly the doctor's words could wipe the smiles right off all of them, maybe for good this time.

> The Lais are having their party today. Can I stay and go?

Her grandma responded almost immediately:

> If it's okay with the Lais, of course you can. I'll pick you up after the party. Love you.

Winnie pushed her blankets off and looked around for her shirt and jeans. They were on top of Pippa's dresser.

"You're awake?" Pippa's voice was groggy and quiet as she slowly picked her head off her pillow, her hair sticking out on all ends. "Where're you going?"

"I'm meeting my grandma at home," Winnie lied as she pulled on her jeans and stuck the money back in her pocket. She hadn't slept much during the night. She made plans instead. "Tell your mom and grandma thanks, okay?"

She'd spent all night googling and figuring everything out. It was easier than she was expecting it to be. She would:

Take the 9:25 a.m. bus from Ocean Avenue to Red Bank.

Take the 10:16 a.m. train from Red Bank to New York Penn Station.

Arrive in the city at 11:46 a.m.

She had enough money in her pocket to get there and back, with $2.75 left over.

The parade was set to kick off at noon at the intersection of Twenty-Fifth Street and Fifth Avenue, which Google Maps said would take Winnie a twelve-minute walk, but she could go to Christopher Street instead, where the parade would turn once they crossed Sixth Avenue (she read all this online, exceptionally thankful that the LGBTQ community made things nice and easy for her to research). Winnie didn't entirely know where all these streets were exactly, but she had her phone and Google Maps and she had to assume she'd be able to follow the crowd inevitably donned in rainbows.

If she followed the parade, she would get to see the Stonewall Inn, and the AIDS Memorial, and everybody—*everybody*—who was celebrating together, marching together and waving flags and cheering, holding each other up.

She wouldn't be going to the hospital. She wouldn't be going to Pippa's party.

She was going to go to Pride.

"Wait, Winnie," Pippa called after her, sitting up in bed.

Winnie paused, hovering in place with her hand on Pippa's bedroom door. "I need to go, Pippa."

"I'm sorry," Pippa said. "About your mom. But I really think you should come to the party later. Lucía and me, we can make sure you have a good time."

Winnie felt all the feelings she had tried to push

down all last night, the same feelings that made her yell at her dad, the same ones she could not keep locked up anymore. "I don't want to go to your stupid party, Pippa! It's not my fault you had terrible friends last year, so just leave me alone!"

It was the second time in less than twenty-four hours that Winnie made Pippa go completely silent. Pippa's face crumpled, and Winnie turned away because she couldn't see it, she could not look at Pippa's face and know that it was her fault. She grabbed her backpack off the floor, and because she couldn't help it, because it was sitting there and Winnie couldn't take her eyes off it and she didn't want to think about how many smiles she'd let slip away ever since they'd found it, she grabbed the sea glass off Pippa's dresser and shoved that into her pocket, too.

Without another moment's hesitation, Winnie left.

SIXTEEN

IT WAS EASIER THAN SHE THOUGHT IT WOULD BE AS SHE SLIPPED
out of Pippa's house, heading up the street toward the
seawall. The air was damp and salty, all morning dew
and ocean breezes, and she walked along the bottom
of the wall, not wanting to draw any attention to herself by climbing.

She had nothing but crumbled dollar bills in one
pocket and sea glass in the other, but the money felt
good. It felt enough. It would get her there, and the
rest would fall into place. It had to. That was the point
of Pride, wasn't it? A community coming together and

being open and loving and not having to worry about anything other than being happy and proud and safe.

A small group of people were waiting by the bus station. There was a metal bench and a small covering and a sign that Winnie used to cross-check with Google Maps and confirm that she was in the right place. She glanced around at the other people waiting. A couple of teenagers. A few men. And one woman with dark hair close to the color of Winnie's.

Winnie wondered if Maria was still going to Pride, or if she would instead spend the day at the hospital with Winnie's mom.

Winnie wondered if her mom was okay.

The bus pulled up. It was big and gray, and it stopped in front of them, bringing a dirty fog of exhaust and sand behind it. When they lined up in a small, haphazard line, Winnie made sure to stay close to the dark-haired woman she stood behind.

The bus doors swung open, and Winnie checked her phone before looking over her shoulder. She half expected Pippa's grandma to come running after her, or for her dad to start calling, demanding she see her mom.

The road was clear. No one called or came for her.

She stood almost too close to the dark-haired woman, throwing up a silent thank-you that the woman didn't seem to notice or mind, and that Winnie was blessed with her dad's tall genes. She didn't hover. She watched carefully and did as everyone else did, paying for the ride and quickly finding a seat. She was right in front of the dark-haired woman, and no one thought it was weird they hadn't spoken once to each other. No one even bothered to take notice that Winnie was actually alone.

Anyway, it didn't matter. The bus doors closed, and they started moving.

Winnie was on her way to Pride.

SEVENTEEN

WINNIE WAS ON THE TRAIN, AND THERE WERE ENOUGH GROUPS of people, enough families, that so long as she hovered close to at least one of them, she was hoping she'd continue to go unnoticed. She made herself as tall as she could, remembering the time she went back-to-school shopping with her mom last year and the woman at the register asked if Winnie was in high school.

"But you're so tall!" she had exclaimed.

Winnie was also the very first girl in her grade to get her period. Seriously, everyone else throughout the fifth and sixth grades came to her with questions as if she were some sort of expert. In fairness, her mom was a little too open and honest and detailed about what was going on inside Winnie's body—and its connection with pregnancies—so she *was* kind of an expert.

Regardless, it was a year of body changes that happened quickly and awkwardly—Winnie's shoe size went from a six to a nine in what felt like a week, making her constantly trip over her feet for months before she got used to it—and she was putting a lot of eggs in that basket now, hoping everyone assumed she was older than she really was.

As the train started moving, most of the people were minding their own business anyway. Winnie's grandma would be pleased.

Winnie tried to mind her own business, too. She stared out the window as the smog-covered buildings of North Jersey went by, leaning forward and pressing her head against the window, trying to see the skyline of the city ahead of them. She kept one hand wrapped around the money in her pocket, and the other held tightly to her phone. No one was looking for her. No one had texted or called or questioned her absence.

Which was good. It was fine. As long as they didn't know, it didn't matter.

Every time they stopped at another train station, Winnie held her breath, hoping that no one would make her get off or turn back around. But they kept going, and no one bothered her, and when the train conductor came around to collect the little pink tickets, Winnie handed him one—one ticket good for a trip from Red Bank to New York Penn Station—and when she purposely looked back at the woman sitting behind her, to try to at least make it look like she was with *someone*, the conductor didn't question it. He took her ticket and punched it and stuck a longer, different, white ticket into the front of her seat.

So far, so good.

The train came to another stop. There were so many stops, and Winnie wished the train would just go so she could get there faster and her heart could stop racing. This time, a loud group of teenagers got on board. The train car Winnie was in had been so quiet, and suddenly it was like someone turned the volume up, as the group of five teenagers practically shouted over their laughter and took their seats at the front of the car. Winnie, though she had been perfectly content to mind her own business, couldn't help but watch them.

One of the teenagers was tall and skinny and wore a pink tutu and rainbow-colored leggings that stretched up his long legs. Another had on jeans and a shirt that said ALL Y'ALL in rainbow colors. A third was dressed in dark colors with rainbow boots, and another one of them, who had short purple hair and donned her own rainbow tutu, was painting a heart on his face.

Winnie couldn't stop staring, could not mind her own business, as the teenagers laughed and the one in the rainbow tutu yelled, "Hold still!" while painting her friend's other cheek.

The kid in the ALL Y'ALL shirt caught Winnie looking. "Hey, girl, you want your makeup done? Caitlin here does the *best* rainbow hearts."

"It's true," Caitlin-with-the-purple-hair confirmed. "I do."

Winnie almost shook her head no. Except . . . she did want her makeup done. She remembered how much she loved the rainbow that Maria put on her face, Maria's fingers warm against Winnie's chin and cheeks. She nodded yes.

"Come over here, then."

She went over to them and they scooted tight

together to make room. Caitlin reached out to tuck Winnie's hair behind her ear so she could hold her chin gently but firmly. Winnie felt like her cheeks were on fire, and she could only hope Caitlin didn't notice as she brought the makeup pen to Winnie's face.

"Don't tag me in any photos on Facebook today," the kid in the rainbow leggings said. "I don't need that kind of attention."

"Who posts on Facebook anyway?"

"Adam's Instagram is linked up to his! I really can't be seen there."

"Are you going to Pride?" Winnie asked, her voice a whisper as Caitlin brought her own face close to work carefully.

"Yeah we are," she said with a wink.

"Me too," Winnie said. "I'm going, too."

Caitlin looked back toward where Winnie had originally been sitting, and Winnie held her breath for a moment. She probably shouldn't have said anything. "What are you, like, fourteen?"

Sure, Winnie could be fourteen. "I'm meeting my friends when I get there. To the city."

Winnie's cheeks flushed even more under Caitlin's

gaze as Winnie lied. Caitlin looked like she was about to say something else, but then the kid with the heart on his cheek, the same one that was currently being drawn on Winnie's, smiled at her. "One of us! Welcome! Enjoy!"

Winnie almost smiled back at him. Or maybe she *did* smile back.

Caitlin finished the heart on Winnie's cheek and then quickly kissed her on the other. Winnie thought she would burst into flame.

"You want to see it?" Caitlin asked.

Winnie nodded, and Caitlin pulled out her phone and put it on selfie mode so Winnie could look at her own face. She had a rainbow heart on her cheek and she really *was* smiling.

Caitlin leaned in, and the others all joined her, as she stretched out her arm and took a photo.

Winnie sat with them for the rest of the train ride.

New York Penn Station was the last stop on the train line, and Winnie's new friends all quickly gathered their things and got up to hover by the doors. Winnie followed them.

"You sure you're good? Your friends are here?" Caitlin asked.

Winnie suddenly had the intense urge to say no, to tell Caitlin the truth. She didn't want them to leave her. She wanted to go with them to Pride and join their circle of friends, all donned in rainbows and smiling and together. Holding each other's hands, just holding each other, period. Winnie didn't want them to go.

But she couldn't tell them the truth, either. She couldn't let them send her home. "Yes," she said. "My friends are here."

There was a lump in her throat when she realized that her friends were actually in Sea Bright, getting ready for Pippa's family's party on the beach. She stuck her hand in her pocket, touching the smooth surface of Pippa's sea glass.

The train doors opened, and Caitlin leaned in to give Winnie another kiss on the cheek. "Maybe we'll see you there, then!" she said. She and the rest of her group exited the doors and got lost in the rush of people.

Winnie was, once again, alone.

Everyone else on the train stood and started lining up and pushing their way out the doors, too, and

Winnie knew she had to follow them, knew she had to get off the train, otherwise someone would definitely realize she was never meant to be on it, but she couldn't get herself to move.

Her heart was thrumming in her chest, into her throat, and she swallowed it down. *This is what you want, Winnie. This is where you're supposed to be.*

She followed the crowd out of the train and into the dank tunnel, making her way up the stairs with the sea of people all going in the same direction: up. Up and out into the New York City streets, where they would diverge into different directions, the business suits and the tourists and the rainbow-colored marchers.

It was easy to know which group of people to follow, but also so easy to get lost. Winnie stepped out of Penn Station and blinked back the bright sun that was suddenly in her face, the way the light reflected off the buildings that towered all around her. Those buildings reached toward a sky that was cloudy and gray even as the sun poked through, a damp heat immediately clinging to Winnie's skin and making her wonder if the heart on her cheek would melt down her face before long.

Winnie got lost staring up at those buildings, as people pushed and shoved and spun around her, her feet heavy and planted on the concrete. There was a line of taxis right in front of her, cars honking as they tried to speed around them, and people were talking and shouting and laughing and yelling and Winnie couldn't differentiate any of it.

She didn't like the fact that, although she could strain her neck and see the skyline of the city from the seawall on clear days (she always knew where to look and that it was there, even on cloudy ones), Winnie could *not* see her home from here. She did not know where it was, didn't even know where to look for it, the water hidden away behind the tall buildings and concrete.

She'd never been this far away from home alone before, away from her family. Away from her mom— who Winnie had left behind in a hospital bed.

Winnie remembered a time when her mom was pregnant—she couldn't remember which time—when her mom was getting ready for the day. She was only in her underwear and a bra, putting lotion on her arms and newly swollen stomach after a shower. Winnie was still in her pajamas, watching TV while sprawled out at the foot of her parents' bed. "Do you want a brother or a sister?" Winnie's mom asked.

Winnie, who had liked girls as long as she could remember, who had been friends with both boys and girls growing up, who couldn't care less about the differences between them, said as much. "I don't care."

"Me either." Her mom thought about it. "I think so anyway. I mean, I want to say it doesn't matter. Gender and sexuality, all of it. It shouldn't matter. You know that, right, Winnie?"

Winnie missed the clarity of that. She wanted more than anything to feel that certainty again—the certainty of her mom, happy and pregnant and smiling—to know that none of it mattered, that she didn't need to hide, that she had family who loved her. Always.

It was time to stop stalling. Winnie would not get that certainty anymore on the other side of the seawall, or in the community center, or at her grandma's house.

She would only get that here.

EIGHTEEN

IT WAS 11:51 A.M., AND THE PARADE STARTED AT NOON, WHICH meant that Winnie needed to move quickly. She wanted to be there for the start of it, and she wanted to follow the parade all the way to the end. She wanted all of it—she didn't want to miss any of it.

She didn't even need to pull out her phone and look for directions. The crowds were rainbows; everyone had color, most had *all* the colors, and the flair and the makeup that Winnie loved, that Winnie wore on her own cheek. There were flags leading the way— rainbow flags, yes, but also the pale pink and blue of the trans flag; the pink, purple, and blue of the bi flag;

and a bunch of other colored flags that Winnie didn't immediately recognize but wanted to look up as soon as she could.

This was her community, on full display, shouting about who they were, celebrating with one another, being proud of who they were and of the community they created and belonged to, and Winnie loved it. She wormed her way into the middle of a large crowd, wanting to be surrounded by those colors and those smiles and that excitement.

And there were enough smiles here for everyone.

They walked for ten minutes, shouting and cheering and some people even dancing their way, and Winnie heard the sound of motorcycles revving not too far ahead of them, followed by loud cheers. She was tall, but not tall enough to see over the people and flags and colors ahead of her, but she had to assume they were close. She had to assume the parade was starting, as people stopped walking forward and instead turned to watch, jumping up and leaning over each other to see.

The motorcycles were decorated in flags. Rainbow flags, trans flags, bi flags. Winnie pushed her way through the crowd to get a closer look, one motorcycle driving right past her with a yellow sign on the back of it that said, PERFECT THE WAY WE ARE! and she remembered when her mom once told her the same thing.

Winnie was never led to believe otherwise, even though she knew a lot of people here had been. Maria didn't realize she liked girls until she was much older than Winnie, but for Winnie . . . it always was just . . . who she was. She never used to think about wanting to hold another little girl's hand, she just *did*.

There was a giant rainbow made of separate smaller balloons being held up by people smiling and waving, and there was a man who was Rollerblading nearly naked—Winnie couldn't help but blush, especially when he winked at her as he held up a sign that said simply LOVE.

Winnie was right up against the gate that separated the people watching from the people marching, and she tried to step up on the bottom rung so that she could be even taller, so that she could see better, leaning over to try to see past the people at her side, who were bouncing and cheering.

"Need help?" a woman standing behind Winnie asked. She was so tall she made Winnie look short, and she was wearing a bright pink dress. Winnie nodded yes, and the woman lifted her by the armpits, like her weight was nothing, so that Winnie could find footing on the top of the gate. The woman held her there, and as a group of marchers walked by, the woman shouted, "Give them five!" and Winnie high-fived all of them.

The floats were gorgeous, the costumes unreal, the music and crowds were loud, the dancers awesome, and Winnie was bummed when the woman behind her had to put her back down. "Gonna head downtown, girl. Enjoy!" the woman said, and then she was gone, and more people were starting to move, too, but Winnie wasn't ready. This was bigger than Asbury Park's Pride. This was bigger than anything Winnie had ever seen, and for the first time in what felt like forever, Winnie couldn't stop smiling. She smiled for the entire parade.

When the tail end of the parade reached the area where Winnie was watching, everyone who was still in the crowd joined the end of it, except for the groups of people who stood around talking or dispersed into nearby bars and restaurants. Winnie stood still, watching the parade disappear down the road, around the corner, leaving confetti and papers and garbage behind that would be cleaned up eventually. There were police cars and officers who lingered in their wake, and

Winnie knew she had to hurry up so that she could go farther downtown, where Caitlin and her friends probably were, where the tall woman who held Winnie up would be, where everyone would be celebrating together and no one would be left out, no one would feel lonely.

The longer she stood there, the quieter it got, and the police officers started removing sections of the gate that had separated the people from the parade.

Everything the parade left in its wake suddenly felt . . . dull. The colors were gone, the laughter moved downtown. It was weird standing there, looking at the street that mere moments before was filled with an energy Winnie loved and was now just . . . empty. It carried on elsewhere, but it would be over there eventually, too. The places it would linger—the bars and clubs and parties—Winnie was too young for those. Winnie couldn't go to those.

Winnie realized Pride was everything she wanted Pride to be, but it couldn't hold her up forever.

"Watch out," a man said, and Winnie startled, realizing he was trying to move the part of the gate she was still leaning against. She stumbled backward, and another man, a cop, took notice of her.

"Hey, where are you supposed to be?" he asked. "Are you lost? You with someone?"

Winnie wasn't lost. She knew exactly where she was—she was where she was supposed to be. But now that the parade was over? She wasn't sure where she was supposed to be now.

Her mom was still back home, in the hospital. Her grandma and dad still wouldn't talk about any of it. Winnie had come to Pride to feel loved and held, and for a bit she did. But what about when it was over? Who would hold her when she went back home?

Winnie was stupid. Winnie was *so stupid*. This fixed *nothing*.

"Seriously, kid, where's your parents? What are you doing here alone?"

Winnie didn't wait for the policeman to ask again, nor did she turn to look at him to attempt to give him an answer. Instead, she mumbled something about meeting someone up the road, avoiding his gaze as she walked away from him. Once she turned the corner, out of view, she took off running.

She ran in the direction of the parade, suddenly surrounded once again by the colors and chanting and cheers and dancing, and it was almost too much. She ran, the colors blurring together as she bumped into people and pushed her way through, running as fast as she could, trying to reach the front of the parade again, trying to start it all over again.

This wasn't the first time Winnie had run away from home. When her mom stopped smiling, Winnie hated being in the house. She hated that her mom shut herself in the bedroom and the house seemed almost too quiet. She hated that her dad kept picking up extra shifts and no one was able to take her on playdates and no one was able to ask about her day.

The night before she'd run away the first time, Winnie's dad told a dumb joke Winnie was barely listening to, didn't even really think was funny. "Winnie doesn't know how to laugh!" he said, and her mom chuckled, actually chuckled, in response. It was small, and wobbly, and not like her usual laughs. But it was real. It happened.

Winnie thought it was a fair trade if her mom got to laugh if Winnie didn't.

The next morning, Winnie packed her backpack and tied her own shoes. She walked around her neighborhood for hours before she got hungry and decided enough was enough and made the long walk back home.

Her mom was shut in her room, sad and tired. Her dad was working.

No one even noticed she'd been gone all day.

Now the front of the parade was too far ahead—everyone was moving too quickly around her. Winnie stopped running, out of breath, feeling her nose start to burn as she fought back tears.

A baby started crying, and Winnie turned to see the baby in their white onesie with a rainbow across their chest, and . . . and was Winnie's own mom still in the hospital? Did her mom lose the baby? Would her mom ever smile again?

She didn't want to be held by these strangers anymore. She wanted her mom to be the one to do it. She just wanted her mom.

Winnie pulled her cell phone out of her pocket to see that she had two texts from Lucía, asking, *What happened? Are you okay?* and *Pippa is really upset, where are you?* and one from her grandma that just said, *Whenever you want to leave Pippa's party, whenever you want to come home, just let me know and I'll come right away.*

Pride was still continuing on around her, but Winnie couldn't breathe.

She didn't feel held. She felt suffocated.

She scrolled through the contact list on her phone and pressed the call button. The phone started ringing, and Winnie leaned up against the wall of a building, her other hand deep in her pocket gripping tightly to Pippa's sea glass, pushing herself away from the people and the dancing and the singing and the laughing, trying not to think of all the smiles and laughter she had thrown away.

There was an answer after only one and a half rings. "Hello? Winnie?"

"Grandma?" Winnie said, her voice cracking. "I need you to come get me."

PART THREE

SUNSHINE (NOUN):

direct sunlight, unbroken by cloud; someone or something (such as a person, condition, or influence) that radiates warmth, cheer, or happiness.

NINETEEN

WINNIE SAT ALONE, THOUGH SHE WAS SURROUNDED BY PEOPLE, on the stairs in Penn Station near gates one through eight for the NJ Transit trains. Everyone was scattered, staring up at the departure board, waiting for the arrival times and tracks for their trains, or sitting around in groups chatting patiently, with suitcases, or backpacks, or coffee cups in their hands.

There were a couple of police officers who kept glancing Winnie's way, but she paid them no mind as she rested her forehead against the railing on the stairs, feeling greasy and sticky and worn. Her cell phone was clamped tightly between her hands so she could feel it vibrate as soon as her grandma arrived.

The rainbow heart on her cheek was probably a sweaty, tear-ruined mess, but it was undoubtedly still there. Her grandma would see her cheek, would see the rainbows scattered about on the flags people were carrying and on the clothes they wore, and she would know why Winnie was here—all before Winnie would be able to open her mouth and explain why on earth she was in New York City by herself, alone, while her mom was in the hospital.

Pride wasn't supposed to make Winnie feel like *this*.

"Winnifred? Winnie!"

Winnie looked up to find her grandma, pale and drained, with windblown, messy hair and wild eyes as she finally spotted Winnie. Winnie stood, using the railing for support, as her grandma ran over to pull her roughly into her arms. She held Winnie tight, and Winnie buried her face in her grandma's chest, trying not to cry. "What is wrong with you? Are you absolutely insane? What were you thinking! How could you . . ." Her grandma continued asking variations of the same question over and over into Winnie's hair.

"I want to go home" was the only thing Winnie could say.

Her grandma pulled back, wiped Winnie's cheeks, brow creasing as she ran her thumb over the smeared makeup on Winnie's skin. "Okay," she said. "Let's go home."

They sat together on the train, making the exact same trip Winnie made to get there, just in reverse. Her seat was even facing backward as they traveled home, and once they emerged from the darkness of the tunnel, she watched the city get smaller and smaller and smaller as they left it behind. Winnie's grandma didn't have much to say, and Winnie didn't want to talk yet anyway. Her grandma typed furiously on her phone, so Winnie had to assume she was texting Winnie's parents, letting them know she was okay, letting them know where she was. Maybe asking about the smeared rainbow on her granddaughter's cheek and the people dressed in rainbows sitting all over the train.

There was a group of teens nearly identical to the ones Winnie rode into the city with—only three of them this time—sitting at the front of their train car. None of them wore rainbows, but they carried flags that Winnie watched them roll up and shove into their open backpacks. One of them pulled out a pack of makeup remover wipes, which she handed to her friend. His face was done up in full makeup, with blue eyelashes and pink lips and rosy cheeks. He pulled out a wipe and started scrubbing his skin. The third of the group was changing his shirt. Winnie couldn't see what the shirt he took off said, but the one he replaced it with was plain.

The one with the makeup scrubbed harder, and the first teenager reached over to help him, and Winnie felt like she might cry.

Actually, Winnie *was* crying.

She wiped her cheeks. The remaining makeup rubbed off onto her hands, and that made her mad. She tried wiping her hands on her jeans, but it wouldn't come off, and Winnie had to clench her jaw, because she didn't want to keep crying, but she couldn't make herself stop, and her chest hurt, and she kicked the seat in front of her, hard.

Luckily there was no one sitting there, but people turned around anyway.

"Winnie." Her grandma's voice was soft. "Are you ready to talk?"

"No," Winnie said.

"I think . . ." her grandma started to say but then stopped. She glanced out the window for a moment, and Winnie thought maybe she decided not to have the conversation at all, that maybe she didn't want to know. But then she turned to look at Winnie and started again. "I think you've had a lot of anger leaking out of you, and piece by piece I'm starting to understand why."

"No," Winnie said again, though she didn't know what she was denying anymore.

The train conductor came around to take everyone's tickets, and Winnie and her grandma fell quiet as he approached. Her grandma handed him their tickets. He punched them and stuck the long white tickets into the back of the seat in front of them before continuing on his way.

"We've spent a lot of time together this summer," Winnie's grandma said. "I mean, I know you hate the clubhouse. And you've been cranky as all hell for most of it. But I thought, you know, we'd spend the summer getting to really know each other, in ways we didn't get a chance to before. I've been a little angry with your mom, that's true, and she and I have a lot of bumps in our relationship we need to work on. But I was happy to have you here so I could get to really know you. You know that, right?"

Winnie shrugged. She *didn't* know. She didn't really know why her mom and grandma fought so much, she didn't know why they couldn't tell her about Winnie's mom's long sad days, she didn't know if her grandma hated Jeanne Strong because she was gay. Winnie didn't even know if her mom was okay—if the baby was . . .

She didn't know anything.

"I want to know you, Winnifred." Her grandma pressed a finger against Winnie's cheek, wiping along the distorted heart. "You're mad your mom is pregnant again. Scared, too, but you mostly keep your mouth shut. And this?" She gestured vaguely around the train. "You've kept your mouth shut about this, too."

"I don't . . . Dad said . . ."

"Talk to me, Winnie."

"I *can't*. I'm not supposed to. You said so, too!" Winnie nearly started shouting. "You said not to tell anyone our business, and Dad said not to say anything about what went on at home before the summer." Winnie took a deep breath to fight back more tears, but she could hear them in her voice anyway. "Mom was so sad, Grandma. She was *so* sad and she never smiled so I tried and save all my smiles for her and I'm scared she's going to never, ever smile again if she loses the baby, and then I'll lose her, too, and I just want . . . I *want* . . ."

Winnie couldn't say anything more. The tears came too fast, and everything in her chest was too tight and she couldn't hold it in anymore. Not the anger or the tears or any of it. She kicked the seat in front of her again. And again. She buried her face in her hands as she cried, loudly, publicly, on a train full of people headed home.

Her grandma wrapped her arms around her and pulled Winnie into her lap, even though Winnie was much too big to be in her grandma's lap, just like she was much too big for her grandma to carry her into the car after her mom had gone to the hospital, but Winnie didn't care. She clung on to her grandma's shirt, and she cried and she cried and she cried, and her grandma cried, too.

Her grandma drove them home from the Red Bank train station, and while Winnie wanted to ask if they were going to go to the hospital, if her mom was still there, if the baby was . . . she hadn't said a word since the train. She was too tired.

But her grandma took them straight home, which left a lot of Winnie's questions still unanswered, though she was also relieved. The last place she wanted to be was the hospital. As they drove through Sea Bright, Winnie watched the seawall that separated the road from the beaches, thinking about Pippa's party, which just felt like a rock swirling around in her stomach. Thinking about Pippa's face when Winnie yelled at her felt like that, too.

Winnie hoped Pippa was having fun. She hoped Lucía was, too. She suddenly missed them so desperately that she sunk into her seat from the weight of it all.

As her grandma turned the car into the opened gate of the community center, Winnie asked, "Is my mom or dad home?" The question startled her grandma, who must have thought Winnie had fallen asleep.

"One more night at the hospital," Winnie's grandma said. "They'll be home tomorrow. We'll wait for them here."

Winnie was exhausted, but her grandma made

her take a shower once they got home anyway, which Winnie thought was fair. She felt grimy, and she supposed after a day on a bus and trains and in the city, she probably was.

What was left of the heart came off in the shower.

When Winnie came out of the bathroom, fresh and pajamaed and tired, her grandma was waiting for her. "You can have my room tonight," she said. "Get some good sleep in a bed."

"I'm gay, Grandma," Winnie said. She couldn't hold anything in anymore. "Did Mom lose the baby?"

"No!" her grandma said, eyes wide, and then shook her head. "I mean. No, your mom didn't lose the baby. I'm so sorry you didn't know that. And the thing about you being gay . . . It's not . . . I don't know why you did all of this instead of just talking to me, but . . ." Her grandma paused, shaking her head, erasing her thoughts, or maybe trying to figure out what those thoughts were. "These are two different conversations, Winnie, you're throwing me off a little."

"Why is my mom still in the hospital? What happened to her?"

"She was clotting. Do you know what a blood clot is? They think that's the reason she lost the others . . .

They have her on blood thinners now, and are keeping her for observation to make sure . . ." Her grandma sighed. "She's not out of the woods, but they think they figured things out. Finally."

They finally figured things out.

Winnie couldn't wrap her head around it. She couldn't wrap her head around these words her grandma was saying to her, because no one had ever taken time to say so much to her about this before. "Can you . . ."

"What?"

"Can you explain it to me? About the blood clots? And the . . . miscarriages?" Winnie asked, the word sounding foreign on her tongue. "Can you tell me what it means?"

Winnie glanced back up at her grandma, who looked as though Winnie took the wind out of *her* lungs, too.

"Yeah," her grandma said. "Come sit with me, and I'll answer your questions. I'll tell you everything I know."

Winnie sat with her grandma as someone explained things to her, without holding back, for the very first time.

TWENTY

WINNIE JOLTED AS SHE WOKE. THE RED NUMBERS ON HER grandma's alarm clock stared at her from the night-stand, reading 11:04 a.m. She realized it had been the sound of the front door opening and closing that woke her. She could hear muffled voices out in the hall through the bedroom door.

It took her a moment to remember where she was, to remember everything that had happened the day before. It felt impossible that it was just one day—that she had snuck out of Pippa's and gone to Pride and called her grandma and sat with her grandma as she explained everything she could to Winnie.

Winnie felt weighed down, sinking into her grand-ma's bed with an ache in her arms and legs and head and neck and everywhere. She felt tired and worn, as if she'd run the New York City Marathon yesterday instead of having just gone to Pride.

Thinking about that, about Pride and the city and the things she had said to her grandma on the train ride and at home made her stomach clench tight, mak-ing every part of her ache even more.

But then Winnie heard the cadence of her mom's voice, muffled through the closed door but clear enough that Winnie would recognize the sound anywhere, and Winnie found herself eager and able to quickly get out of bed. The weighted feeling turned into a feeling of *need* right in Winnie's chest. She needed to see if her mom was okay.

Still, she hovered by the door, hand wrapped around the cool metal of the doorknob, afraid of what she might find on the other side. As she slowly turned the knob, pushing the door open, she heard her grandma say, "I just don't understand why you wouldn't tell me how bad things got. I would have been there for you. I want to be there for you *and* for Winnie, and—" The door creaked as Winnie pushed it open wider, causing her grandma to stop and for all heads—her grandma's, her dad's, and her mom's—to turn and look right at her.

Winnie's mom was sitting on the couch, on Winnie's bed, surrounded by Winnie's blankets. Her eyes seemed huge, and her face was pale. She looked small as she smiled a little smile at Winnie. "Winnie, baby," she said. She looked scared, and Winnie wasn't sure if she was afraid because of the baby and her hospital visit or because of Winnie herself. "Baby," she said again, her voice raw and raspy. "What were you thinking?"

About going to Pride or telling Grandma everything? Winnie wondered.

"You could have been seriously hurt, or lost, Winnie," her dad chimed in from where he was pacing across from where her mom was sitting. "We could have *lost* you, Winnie."

His voice cracked, and it seemed to crack Winnie's mom, too, who started quietly crying, tears streaming from her already reddened eyes. "Come sit with me, Winnie," she said. "We need to talk about this. We need to . . . *I* need to . . ."

Winnie didn't know what *she* needed. She wanted

her mom, she did, she wanted her mom to hold her and she wanted her mom to say that everything was okay and she would keep smiling her big, beautiful smile forever and she would never shut herself behind her bedroom door again and Winnie and her dad would never have to shout at each other in a hospital waiting room again and that next year they would go to Pride together, all of them.

But Winnie was tired, and achy, and mad. For all the ways she wanted her mom to hold her, for all the ways she wanted her dad to say he was sorry, Winnie wanted them to leave her alone. She wanted to scream at them to just leave her alone.

She didn't know which she wanted more. She didn't know what she needed more.

She looked over at her grandma. Maybe she would know.

"You don't need to do that," Winnie's mom said. "You don't need to look at her for . . . Winnie, I'm right *here*. Whatever you need, *I'm* right here."

"No, you're not," Winnie said, finding her voice, surprised at how mean it sounded. "You're not, you're not, *you're not*."

"Winnie," her mom said, and then repeated it:

"Winnie." She was crying harder now, and Winnie realized she was crying hard herself, too, and her dad's eyes were wide and red and wet with tears, too. Her parents looked so young, and scared, especially when Winnie's mom looked over at her grandma, searching for the same guidance Winnie was, and Winnie's grandma seemed so strong and sturdy, suddenly, and Winnie didn't think she looked old at all. She just looked capable of holding them all on her shoulders, even if she was just as tired as the rest of them.

She came up to Winnie, her hands holding on to Winnie's arms and squeezing gently. "Tell them what you need to, Winnie. Tell them everything you told me, and anything else you're keeping locked up."

Winnie's mom tried to get up from where she was sitting on the couch, but she took a deep breath through her nose and stayed where she was instead. Winnie glanced over at her dad, and then warily back at her grandma. "I'm not supposed to."

"I'm telling you right now, Winnie," her grandma said, hands squeezing harder against Winnie's shoulders. "You have permission to say whatever the hell you want. As a matter of fact, you don't need my permission at all. Go sit with your mother and tell her every single thing you need to."

It felt like every one of them was holding their breath in the seconds between her grandma speaking and Winnie deciding what she wanted to do. She hesitated—a lot—but she wanted her mom. *She wanted her mom.* She made her way to the couch, to her mom's arms, and her mom wrapped her up tight, holding her as close as Winnie could get without actually being in her lap, because there was still an entire pregnancy between them. "Talk to me, Winnie. Please," her mom said, and Winnie still didn't know where, or how, to begin.

Her dad came to kneel beside them, and both he and her mom were looking at her with those big, scared eyes, and Winnie was scared, too, because this all felt too heavy. "I don't want you to stop smiling again," Winnie quietly admitted. "What if I say something that makes you stop smiling again?"

The room seemed so quiet, except for her mom's breathing. In, and out, and in again, and out again, as she looked Winnie straight in the eyes and wiped Winnie's cheek. She took another big breath—in and out—and turned to look at Winnie's dad and grandma. "We're going to talk about everything. I'll tell you anything. You do not have to be afraid of making me sad again. That had nothing to do with you, and you couldn't have changed it, and I don't have all the answers here and maybe that's my fault, too, but Winnie, I love you. I'm so, so sorry."

Winnie's dad was crying more now, too, as he added, "I'm sorry, too. I didn't know what to do. I'm sorry."

"Talk to them, Winnifred," Winnie's grandma said again.

"I don't know how," Winnie said.

"I don't know how, either," Winnie's mom admitted. She looked over at Winnie's grandma again, and Winnie thought maybe her mom sometimes needed to feel held, too. Maybe her mom needed *her* mom sometimes, too, even though they didn't know how to understand each other.

"Maybe we should find someone to help with that, then," Winnie's dad said.

"We can't afford that," Winnie's mom said, almost a whisper. "You looked back when . . . your insurance doesn't . . ."

"Let's talk about that together, then," Winnie's

grandma interrupted. "Because I think that sounds like a good place to start."

Winnie's parents and her grandma needed to talk, too. They needed to discuss things without Winnie that they needed to deal with alone as adults. But this time, they weren't purposely hiding anything from Winnie. They would keep talking to her, they said. And they would find a therapist for all of them to talk to, too.

Winnie wasn't sure how her family would bring their inside business all the way outside to a stranger. But they wanted to. And Winnie wanted to, too. And maybe her grandma was right. They had to start somewhere, and Winnie wasn't sure yet where exactly that might be.

She showered, and her grandma made her lunch, a sandwich that sat on a paper plate in her lap as she swung on her grandma's porch swing, looking out at the seawall, while her family continued talking inside. She couldn't see over the wall from where she sat, and she thought maybe that was for the best. She wasn't ready to see the city.

She hadn't thought she was hungry, but suddenly she was almost finished. It had been a while since she last ate, she supposed, and she brushed the crumbs off her jeans.

"You look forlorn, as always."

Winnie looked up and saw Jeanne Strong making her way up Winnie's grandma's driveway, a book, as usual, in her hand. Winnie sighed. Jeanne Strong might not have been the *last* person Winnie wanted to see, but she was definitely up there on the list. "I *feel* forlorn," Winnie said. "That's why I look this way."

"I heard you took yourself on an adventure yesterday," Jeanne said as she stood in front of Winnie, blocking the sun and casting shade over Winnie's seat.

"My grandma told you that?" Winnie asked, stunned her grandma would tell Jeanne Strong anything so personal.

"She asked me to be on standby in case your mom or dad needed anything. You had us all in a tizzy at the clubhouse. Even Liam Porter seemed worried." Jeanne winked. "I also may have had to explain to your grandma exactly what Pride was. I forget how old your Maude is sometimes, but seriously, she has a TV. She has a smart phone. She has a granddaughter I'm sure she'd like to learn these things from."

Winnie glared at Jeanne. She wasn't dumb; she knew exactly what Jeanne was trying to do. "My mom was afraid my grandma would hurt my feelings if she found out. How do you know she won't?"

"Your grandma used to cook for my wife all the time, you know," Jeanne said. "When she got sick, and I had to work during the day. She hated being lonely. Your grandma made sure she wasn't. They were close."

"I thought my grandma didn't like you," Winnie said, then felt her cheeks turn warm. "I mean . . ."

Jeanne waved her off. "You meant what you said. And I meant what I said. Maude and my wife were close. They were good friends. Your grandma and I have never gotten along, regardless of how much Peggy tried to force us to."

"Why do you think my mom was scared for me to tell my grandma, then?"

"That's something you'll have to talk to your mom about."

"We're going to talk to a therapist. My mom and dad and grandma and me."

"That sounds very smart."

"Were you really married?" Winnie didn't know why she asked it. Jeanne moved to sit next to Winnie on the porch swing, and the sun shone brightly again in Winnie's eyes.

"Yeah," Jeanne said. "Well, no. Well, yes. It was a civil union. This was a long time ago. Do you know much about our history, Winnie? I know it's so much better for you young ones these days—I mean, look at you! You're all of ten years old and know who you are more than I did at thirty!"

"I'm twelve," Winnie said. "And my mom's best friend, Maria, says the same thing. That she didn't even know until she was a lot older."

Jeanne nodded. "It's important you remember, though. That things weren't always as easy." She paused, tilted her head, thinking. "Not that it's perfectly easy now. I know that. I won't trivialize your feelings."

Winnie didn't really know what to say to that. "Thank you."

"Here," Jeanne said, giving Winnie the book she'd been holding.

Winnie tried not to roll her eyes. She took it, glancing at the bright cover. Two girls looking at each other on a roller coaster. Winnie traced the shiny *Stonewall Honor Book* sticker in the corner.

She was suddenly glad she hadn't rolled her eyes, because she loved it. She loved the way those two girls were smiling at each other, the same way she was realizing she wanted to smile with Lucía. *"Almost Flying?"*

"I did some research," Jeanne said. "It's a book for your age group. I thought it might help you to read about queer girls your own age."

Winnie traced the cover with her fingers. "Thank you," she said again, meaning it.

"You're so resistant to help," Jeanne said. "And I know I come on, well, strong, but when you're ready, or you want to talk, don't forget that I'm here. For all the pain, there's a support team out there for you. There are people who want to be in your corner no matter what. You have to let them, Winnie. Trust me on that."

Winnie thought about Maria, who lied to her mom and grandma to take Winnie to Asbury Pride, because it was important to Winnie and Maria understood that. She thought about Lucía, who was afraid of what her family might think if they knew she liked girls, and how much lighter Lucía seemed just being able to talk to Winnie about it. She thought of Pippa, who held her hand on the beach as they watched a movie when

Winnie admitted out loud to her new friends for the first time, "I'm gay."

They were the people to hold her up when things inside her home made her feel like she was sinking to the ocean floor.

"Thank you," Winnie said again.

She looked up at Jeanne Strong and smiled at her for the very first time.

TWENTY-ONE

JUST BECAUSE THEY HAD A LOT TO THINK AND TALK ABOUT, AND just because Winnie's feelings were important and valid, that did not mean she wasn't in trouble for hopping a bus and a train and running away, so said Winnie's grandma.

Which is why Winnie was standing outside of Pippa's house, begrudgingly ringing the doorbell so she could *apologize to Mrs. Lai for betraying her trust and generosity and for lying.* Again, so said Winnie's grandma.

It was fair, Winnie supposed. But she didn't really care about apologizing to Mrs. Lai.

She really cared about talking to Pippa, which was why she stood there, feeling small, rolling Pippa's sea glass around in her pocket.

Grace Lai answered the door. "I should have expected Maude would send you over," she said, which would have made Winnie feel chagrin if Pippa's grandma weren't smiling.

"I'm sorry for betraying your trust and generosity and for lying," Winnie said. "Is Pippa's mom home? I want to tell her I'm sorry for betraying *her* trust and generosity and for lying."

"I'll give her the message," Grace Lai said. "Thank you for coming over and telling us that. I imagine you have a lot going on at home, and so long as you don't betray our trust and generosity ever again, you are always welcome here, Winnifred."

She was being so nice that Winnie really did feel chagrin. "I really am sorry. I promise I won't ever do it again."

"We missed you at the party the other day. You know, Pippa is at the pool club with that other little girl. I imagine you have some things you'd like to say to my granddaughter, too," Grace Lai said.

She wasn't wrong. Still, Winnie blushed.

All things considered, and especially since Winnie's grandma told her she was to apologize to the Lais and then head right home, Winnie probably should have done just that. All things considered, Winnie decided to at least text her grandma to let her know that she was walking to the pool club to talk to Pippa and that she promised she'd be home immediately after.

Her grandma responded that if she wasn't home within the hour, she was going to call the police and send out a search party and when they found her she would never be allowed to leave the house again.

All things considered, Winnie figured that was fair.

It was a hot, humid, sticky day, so it was no surprise that the pool was full of bobbing heads and splashing hands, of kids and babies in floaties and adults wading in the small amount of room they had. Winnie spotted Lucía before she could find Pippa. Lucía was sitting along the edge of the pool as always, wearing a sweat-and-splash damp white shirt as she slowly kicked her legs in the water. Even though Winnie knew Pippa had to be somewhere right by Lucía's feet, the pool was so full she couldn't spot her.

But then, suddenly, like a life preserver, Pippa popped out of the water, right by Lucía's feet, her black hair floating around her as she buoyed and bobbed, laughing. Lucía was laughing, too, and Winnie didn't know what they were laughing about but she had this tightness in her chest, because she wanted to know. She wanted to be laughing with them.

She wanted to give them her smiles and laughter.

When she made her way over to where Lucía was sitting, taking a seat beside her friend, the laughter stopped. "Hi," Winnie said, when all Pippa and Lucía did was stare at her like fish.

"Hi," Lucía said. Her smile was small, but it still made it easier for Winnie to breathe.

Winnie swung her feet in the water in time with Lucía's, but Pippa said nothing and didn't look at Winnie, either. "How was the party?" Winnie asked.

Which apparently was the wrong thing to say. "You *lied* to me," Pippa said, her voice tight and cracked. She grabbed the ledge between Winnie's and Lucía's legs, holding on so tightly her water-wrinkled knuckles turned white. "You yelled at me and you lied to me. I was worried about your mom. But my grandma said *your* grandma said you ran away to New York City."

"Is your mom okay?" Lucía asked.

Winnie didn't know who to answer. She wanted

to avoid answering them both, but not talking about things was what got her in this entire mess to begin with. "I'm sorry. I wanted to go to New York City Pride because Maria told me that our entire community would be there, and they would be happy, and they would take care of each other, and hold each other, and I just . . . needed that. My mom's okay. The baby I think is okay? My grandma says . . . well, it doesn't matter. But so far the baby is okay. My mom's scared and sad, and so is my dad, and so am I, which is why I didn't want to tell you she was pregnant. She's been pregnant before. Those babies didn't make it."

Neither Pippa nor Lucía responded.

"I know your party meant a lot to you. I only asked how it went because, well, I hope you had fun, is all," Winnie said, and then quietly added: "I wish I went."

Pippa shifted her hands until she was touching Winnie's leg. "I wish you were there, too. It wasn't the same without you." She looked up at Winnie with the big, beautiful eyes that used to make Winnie blush before they became friends. "We're your best friends, Winnie. You should tell us things. We'd take care of you, too."

Lucía nodded.

"I'm sorry," Winnie said again. "I didn't think I could. And, I don't know. I wasn't sure how? It was all really confusing."

Pippa pressed her hands flat against the ledge of the pool, pulling herself up and out, water dripping off her and onto both Winnie and Lucía as she sandwiched herself between her friends.

"Did you really go all the way to the city by yourself?" Pippa asked, and it sounded exactly like forgiveness and how best friendship should, taking a tremendous weight off Winnie's shoulders. "My mom freaked out once when my older cousin and I rode one subway stop by ourselves. One! How did you even know where you were going? I'd have gotten so lost."

"Me too," Lucía said. "I would get on the wrong train or something before I even made it to the city. I've never even *been* to the city."

"I googled." Winnie shrugged. "And I got lucky."

"Don't you dare run away ever again," Pippa said, wrapping a wet arm around Winnie's dry shoulders. "At least not without telling us first. We won't go with you, but we'd sure as heck talk you out of it."

Winnie reached into her pocket to pull out the sea glass. "I took this from you. I'm sorry. It's okay if you don't want it back, though."

Pippa didn't hesitate. She took it right out of Winnie's palm. "I want it. I definitely want it." She turned to Lucía. "We'll need to find you one, too! That way we all have a piece of sea glass, the three of us."

They sat quietly together, as Pippa cradled her sea glass in her hands, and people swam and splashed around them. Someone ran by, and the lifeguard blew her whistle to tell them to stop running, and Winnie leaned her head up to the sky, letting the sun warm her face as she closed her eyes and enjoyed it.

"How was Pride?" Lucía interrupted quietly.

Winnie couldn't help but smile. "You'd have loved it."

She opened her eyes to see Lucía smiling, too—a big, beautiful smile that felt almost like a secret shared between them—but it didn't last long. Lucía looked away, down at her toes in the pool water as that smile slowly faded.

It made Winnie think about what Jeanne Strong said, about support systems and allowing people in your corner, because you'll need them.

Before Winnie could let all the thoughts in her head stop her, she channeled the little girl she once was, the one who got caught kissing girls on the playground, the one who always wanted to hold another little girl's hand, the one who hadn't ever been told she couldn't do those things outside of her home.

She leaned in, over Pippa, and kissed Lucía's cheek.

When she pulled away, Lucía was blushing.

But she was also smiling again.

Lucía needed Winnie in her corner, and Winnie could do that. She could make sure that Lucía felt supported and held while she figured out who she was and what that meant for her and her relationship with her family.

Winnie *wanted* to be the one to make Lucía feel supported and held.

Lucía's hand was resting behind Winnie's back, palm flat on the concrete next to Pippa's, as Pippa was also leaning back on her palms. Winnie reached back to place one hand on top of Lucía's and the other on top of Pippa's, as the three of them sat together in the sun.

"You both should come with me to book club," Winnie suddenly said.

"At the clubhouse?" Pippa asked. "Count me in!"

"Me too," Lucía added.

"Good," Winnie said, sighing softly. Liam Porter would absolutely hate it when they all showed up, books in hand, ready to discuss. "I think I'll really like that."

Maria was walking out of Winnie's grandma's house just as Winnie was making her way up the driveway. She smiled wide when she saw Winnie, and Winnie found herself walking faster, wanting to close the distance between them as quickly as possible.

Maria's arms were open wide for Winnie to fall right into. "I was just visiting your mom, seeing if she needed anything. She went to lie down, though. I'm glad I got to see you before I left."

"Me too," Winnie said. "I'm glad to see you, too."

"I heard you went to Pride without me. You're not allowed to disappear on us, by the way." Maria winked, but then grew serious. She ran her fingers along Winnie's cheek. "If I knew how desperately you wanted to go . . . I'd have moved mountains to make that happen. Don't you know that?"

Winnie nodded, looking down at her toes. She had Pippa and Lucía, but while Maria had been her mom's best friend for years and years before Winnie was even born . . . she was Winnie's favorite person, too. Maria was always in Winnie's corner—she had been holding Winnie up her entire life. "Take me next year," Winnie said, and quickly added: "And my friend Lucía, too. Promise me."

Maria held her close again. "Always, Winnie."

Maria started to leave, and Winnie watched from her grandma's porch stoop as she made her way down the driveway. "Maria, wait!"

"Yeah?" Maria said, turning back to look at her.

"You make me happy when skies are gray, too," Winnie said. "I just wanted you to know that."

The smile Maria gave her was stunning.

Inside, Winnie found her grandma in the kitchen, staring at Winnie's mom's tablet as she leaned against the counter, using her finger to scroll. Her grandma looked up and motioned for Winnie to come and join her. "I'm just looking for dinner ideas for the week. I'll need to get more groceries if your mom is staying for a few days," she said, before pushing the tablet aside and focusing solely on Winnie.

Winnie flushed a little under the attention. "Maria said Mom's lying down?"

Her grandma nodded. "She's okay, just tired. Which is why I'm glad she's not rushing to get back home, especially with your dad working full days. She's on new meds from the doctor to hopefully keep her blood from clotting, and she's a little stressed about everything. Which is okay," her grandma added when Winnie felt herself cringing. "She's going to be stressed and worried and sad. We're going to keep an eye on her, Winnifred. We'll get her the help she needs. Meanwhile, it gave me and Maria some time to chat."

Well, *that* surprised Winnie. "You and *Maria*?"

"I had some questions. I have some questions for you, too," Winnie's grandma said. "Maria has known parts of you for what seems like forever. Parts that I've just found out about."

Now Winnie was sure her cheeks were bright red. "Oh."

"I know your mom had concerns about me. Concerns that went back to when she was younger. I didn't always try and get to know her growing up, though she didn't always let me, either. But that's on the two of us." Winnie's grandma reached across the kitchen island that separated them to tap gently under Winnie's chin, getting Winnie to look back up to meet her eyes. "I want to know more about you, Winnie. I'll admit it hurts a little that you didn't think I would want to. Did you think I'd . . . ?"

Her grandma didn't finish the question, but Winnie thought about her answer anyway. "I thought, maybe, I guess. But Jeanne Strong told me you were really good friends with her wife."

Her grandma shook her head, mumbling, "Jeanne Strong needs to mind her own business."

Despite the seriousness of the conversation, and the squirmy feeling it brought to Winnie's stomach, she couldn't help but smile at the familiarity of her grandma's words.

"I want to know all of you, Winnifred," her grandma said again. "It's been nice having you close. And, I might not understand everything. I might have a lot of questions. But I want to try, and I want you to trust me to try, too."

"I like girls, Grandma," Winnie said. "I've always liked girls."

There was a pause, a moment during which Winnie

could tell her grandma was trying to decide what to say next.

"When I first met Pippa," Winnie found herself saying, "I used to blush all the time. I was so worried everyone could tell, that you could tell. But she was so pretty. She *is* so pretty, but she's my friend now, so it's different." Winnie thought some more. "Lucía has a really pretty smile. It's beautiful, like Mom's."

"You have your mom's smile, you know."

Winnie paused. She didn't know that.

She didn't like thinking about sharing her mom's smiles. They were her mom's, and her mom needed them.

"Grandma?"

"Yes, Winnifred?"

Winnie glanced over at the couch, where her blankets were all bunched up and messy, even though her grandma told her that morning (and every other morning) to fold them nicely. She never folded them, like she never used to make her bed when she had one. It made the couch feel more like hers. It made the living room feel owned and lived in. Winnie was getting used to that couch, to her grandma waking her up, clanging around in the kitchen. To being the last one awake at night, after her grandma went to sleep and Winnie was left to turn out the light.

"How long is mom staying with us?" she asked. "How long am I . . . staying?"

Her grandma sighed. "I'm not entirely sure. The plan was for you to stay until the end of the summer."

It was almost July. Which meant there were two months until school started in September. Two months until the baby might come in September. Two months.

Winnie didn't know what might change during those two months.

She didn't know if she would be ready.

"But you'll still be here, right? After we go home, you'll come visit? Or I can come here?" Winnie asked. "I like being here with you, and I don't want to go back to how it was before, and I think I want to come back next summer, too. If that's okay?"

Her grandma smiled, reaching out to take Winnie's hand in her own, squeezing. "You'll be sick of me come next summer. And, Winnie, you can stay as long as you need, and you can come back whenever. I mean that."

Winnie smiled, breathing easier. "It'd be nicer if I had a bed."

"Yes, well, you'll have to make do."

"And I still hate the clubhouse."

Her grandma laughed.

Through the laughter, Winnie heard her grandma's bedroom door creak open, and she turned to find her mom, eyes bleary but bright, as she leaned against the doorframe and smiled a small smile at Winnie. "Hey, you."

"How are you feeling?" Winnie asked.

Her mom looked behind Winnie at Winnie's grandma, before making eye contact again with Winnie. "The baby is moving around awkwardly in there. It feels better to be on my feet right now. Will you take a walk with me?"

Winnie wanted to ask if her mom should be taking walks, and if the baby moving around awkwardly was a good or bad thing, and a million other things that had been circling her mind that Winnie had been too scared to ask.

"It's good for me to walk around, just not too much," her mom answered one of Winnie's unspoken questions. "We'll just take a really slow, short walk outside."

Winnie glanced down at her mom's stomach, then up into her mom's eyes. "Okay."

TWENTY-TWO

THEY WALKED ACROSS THE STREET, TO THE SEAWALL THAT Winnie loved. Winnie's mom held tight to Winnie's hand, allowing support as they headed toward the staircase that climbed up and over the seawall, providing access to the beach.

Winnie reached for the smooth wood banister of those stairs, much different from the rough and uneven rock she usually climbed. Winnie stood as strong and steady as she could make herself as her mom held on to her arm and the railing, and they climbed.

Winnie's mom wanted to put her feet in the sand. Winnie wanted to do whatever made her mom happy.

On the other side of the seawall, with their feet in the sand and the expansive ocean spread out before them—the city skyline somewhere invisible in the distance, the sun too bright and the sky too hazy to see much of anything—Winnie and her mom stood, close together and quiet until Winnie's mom said, "We should talk about the baby."

Winnie, standing in the bright sunshine on a public beach covered in colorful umbrellas that popped out of the sand like flowers, surrounded by people sunbathing and running and jumping into the water, and seagulls trying to steal picnic food, as well as all the other sounds of the summer . . . did not want to talk about the baby. "Mom?"

"Yeah?"

"What did you think about when you were sad? When you didn't come out of your room and didn't smile?"

Her mom got really quiet. A large wave crashed against the wet sand—a few smaller kids who had been playing along the edge of the water began screaming and running away. Winnie's mom's hand was holding on so tightly.

Winnie pushed forward. "Did you ever think of me?"

Her mom closed her eyes. "Oh, Winnie. I'm so sorry—"

"I tried really hard to save all my smiles up for you," Winnie interrupted. "Because you started smiling again and I tried to do anything I could to make sure you didn't stop. I thought maybe if I didn't smile or laugh then I could make sure to smile and laugh with you, so that you could have them, and then you could keep smiling, and so I wouldn't have to lose you again."

Winnie's mom was shaking. Winnie wanted to ask her if they should turn back, if they should be sitting down in the air-conditioned home instead of standing here in the blinding summer sun, staring at the busy beach, talking about things they had spent so long *not* talking about. But Winnie was also afraid that if they went inside, all the things she wanted her mom to talk about would get locked away again.

They were outside, and they were talking about it. Winnie didn't want to do anything to change that now.

"I don't know how to talk to you about my depression," her mom said.

Winnie held her breath. It was the first time anyone had used that word.

"I don't know how to talk to you about the miscarriages and how awful I felt. How empty. I know you were there and I know it hurt you, all of it hurt you. But I don't know how to talk to you about this."

"Dad says that's what the therapist is for."

"I want to talk to you, though," Winnie's mom said. "I don't want to make the mistakes me and my mom did, and I don't want you to ever feel like I sometimes do. Do you think I'm selfish, Winnie? For locking you out? For trying again and again and again to have this baby?"

Did she?

Sometimes it made Winnie angry. Sometimes her chest felt tight and her stomach hurt and she just wanted to scream.

But did she think her mom was selfish? "I don't know," Winnie said honestly. "Lucía says her mom says that even though she had so many babies, it doesn't mean she loves any of the older ones any less. That her wanting more didn't mean that she wasn't already happy. But . . ."

"But what, Winnie?" her mom asked. "Tell me. Please."

"I don't really understand why you keep trying. It makes you so sad. It makes everyone so scared and sad." Winnie wiped the sweat off her forehead. Her mom was red and sweaty, too. "We should go back to grandma's."

"I want it so bad, Winnie," her mom said, staring out at the ocean. "I feel like a failure. I feel like I can do this. I feel like I want more than anything to do this. I feel like we deserve it. I know none of that might make sense to you, I know that it's confusing. I just know that I want this so bad, Winnie. But I love you more than anything. You've never been less than enough. You've always been more than. I just . . . need this, too."

"Maria says I'm the sunshine baby."

"What?"

"I know. It's stupid."

Winnie watched as her mom placed her hands on her stomach, rubbing gently against the way her belly—the baby—pressed against her shirt, straining the fabric. Winnie reached out for a moment, to put her hand on top of her mom's hand on top of her stomach, but hovered awkwardly in the space between them instead.

"You can touch, Winnie."

Winnie looked up at her mom, who reached for Winnie's hand. Winnie tensed for a moment, nervous that she was going to make Winnie feel the baby, and Winnie still wasn't sure if she wanted to.

But her mom just held her hand, clasped in both of her own. "Please don't save up your smiles. Not for me. Not for anyone. You smile for you, Winnie. You keep smiling for you. And we'll get help, as a family, so that we can all keep smiling, too."

Winnie's mom wrapped her arm around Winnie's shoulder, and Winnie wrapped her arm right back around her, holding just as tightly, even with the baby bump between them. It didn't matter. She got close enough anyway. "Grandma knows I like girls. And I don't think you should name the baby an old person's name like mine. The people at the senior citizen center didn't realize I wasn't old like them when I signed up for book club, you know."

Winnie's mom laughed, and it was a beautiful sound that stood out among the crashing waves and seagulls and beachgoers. Her smile was beautiful, and Winnie smiled back, the biggest smile she could remember in a long, long while. "I'd like to hear all about that," Winnie's mom said. "I'd like to hear all about your book club, and your new friends, and your big trip to the city."

"Okay," Winnie said. "Maybe me and Grandma can teach you canasta."

"Oh, I think I hate canasta," Winnie's mom said.

Winnie shrugged. "I think I hate it, too."

"We should head back," Winnie's mom said, and Winnie agreed, but neither one of them moved. Her mom whispered, in a voice so soft Winnie was surprised she could even hear her, "Well, maybe just a few more minutes."

When they did finally make their way back home, Winnie's grandma was sitting on the porch swing, waiting for them. Her mom went inside to shower, and as Winnie sat down next to her grandma, close, her grandma wrapped an arm around her, rocking them softly.

"Pippa thinks I'll make a good big sister," Winnie said into the quiet summer air.

"I think she's right," Winnie's grandma replied.

"Do you think at the clubhouse they'd let me and Pippa and Lucía in book club?"

"They'd better," her grandma said. "Anything for you, kid."

"Can we invite Jeanne Strong over for pizza sometime?"

Her grandma laughed. "Don't push it."

"Does that mean no pizza?" Winnie asked, and her grandma used her hand to tickle Winnie's side.

"Someone used all our pizza money," her grandma said.

Winnie laughed. Her grandma smiled.

"Guess we're gonna have to play some canasta to win it all back," Winnie said.

They sat together, looking out at the seawall. Winnie couldn't see the city skyline over it, but she didn't mind. She didn't need to squint and look for it, wishing she was there instead of here.

Being here, held by her grandma, was just fine right now.

ACKNOWLEDGMENTS

I started writing this book long before some of my others were published, and the only reason it will be on the shelves for my readers is because of Jim McCarthy. Jim, thank you for making me believe in my sad characters and their sad books, for not letting Winnie fall to my own insecurities, for championing me and my work. You are the best partner I could ask for in all of this.

To my editor, Krestyna Lypen, I've said this once (twice? Three times?) and you've yet to give me a reason to stop: I've never had to think twice about trusting work in your hands. Thank you for making it easy to take a sad, queer story for middle graders—during a time when such books are being challenged and targeted—and putting that book into the world.

Everyone at Algonquin: Thank you again, and again, and again, for always making me feel safe with you all, and for continuing to usher these books into the world with such determination and care.

Andrew Sass, I don't know how I ever wrote a book without you in my corner. Thank you for always being the best partner in crime and writer buddy anyone could ask for.

Minna Zallman Proctor, I should have dedicated a book to you ages ago for teaching me how to dig deep so that I can tell the truth while making it bearable. Luckily, I've learned more as your colleague than I even did as your student, and all the parts of this book that are *me* are because of you.

To the rest of the faculty and students at the Fairleigh Dickinson MFA program: Thank you for listening to me read an early draft of this in the buttery at Wroxton on that foggy, muggy night in England, and for inspiring me to keep working, keep writing, keep fighting.

To my family: Thank you for always having my back and reading my stories (including my brother and dad, who most days would rather not read at all). (I almost deleted this because it felt rude, but it's also true and I appreciate your constant support.)

As always, a shout-out to my wife, Liz: You are forever my Theo and my wuffenloaf. I would not have gotten through this year without you.

And, most importantly, to every single middle schooler who has reached out to me to tell me your story: I hear and see you, and I always will.